SECRETS BURIED

A LAKE MINNETONKA COZY MYSTERY
BOOK ONE

LYSSA LUND

WHIMSEY PUBLISHING

THANK YOU

Thank you for reading my books! I know you have so many choices and I am honored you have chosen to read mine.

As an independent author I really depend on your reviews to help new readers take a chance on my work. If you enjoy Petals Of Peril it will help so much if you can take a few minutes to leave a review.

Amazon is preferred if it is possible for you to do so. Goodreads and Bookbub are helpful too.

Happy reading!

xoxo, Lyssa

Dedicated to The Moostery Trippers!

CHAPTER 1

"Yes, Cynthia, I got this." Veronica ended the call with a sigh, smoothing back her dark blonde hair from her forehead and forcing a smile. Covering for one of her agents on her day off was not the relaxation she'd planned, but as the owner of her little real estate brokerage, that came with the territory. Glancing up, she took in the building before her, her lips bunching to one side. It would take a special person to be willing to take on an old, run-down project house like this one. *Wow, this needs a lot of work.*

Her gaze ran over the old wood paneling, the dry, cracked paint, and the loose tiles on the roof. It was hard to believe someone had lived here until last month, but then again, from what she knew, the old man had been just as stubborn as this old place seemed to be.

"And there are two interested parties already?" Eyebrows lifting in surprise, Veronica mentally shrugged.

There's a buyer for every house...

"Hi, I'm guessing you're waiting for me?"

Putting on her usual confident smile, Veronica lifted her

head and stuck out one hand as someone came towards her, squinting a little in the bright sunshine. "Yes, I'm Veronica. You were supposed to meet Jess today, but she's a little under the weather."

His handshake was firm, but with his baseball cap and shades, she couldn't make out his face. "And you must be…."

Ugh! I didn't even look at his name.

Dropping her gaze to her cell phone again, she swiped through the document Cynthia had sent her, only for the man to chuckle.

"I'm Chase. Thanks for showing up on short notice, Veronica. I sure appreciate it."

Something was familiar in his tone, something that she couldn't quite make out, and, flashing him a quick smile and ignoring the nervous twirl in her stomach, Veronica gestured to the house. "Shall we step inside?"

"Sounds good." Holding out both hands and spreading his arms wide, Chase let out a long sigh. "Isn't this place great?"

Veronica blinked. *Doesn't sound like I'll have to do much convincing.* "It sure has a lot of potential!"

"Yes, it does." Stepping aside, he waited for her to unlock the front door and then followed her inside. Veronica gestured to the space, her trained eye taking in all the old features of the house that *could* be preserved if someone wanted, but most people these days ripped down and built new. *He could be a classic fix-and-flip kind of guy.*

"I'm happy to let you look around on your own, or we can go through the house together?"

Her throat tightened suddenly as he removed his cap and shades, leaving her melting inwardly with shock. His name threw itself back at her, and she caught it tightly, her heart beginning to pound.

Chase. Chase Lawson. Oh no.

"I'll take it from the look on your face, you recognize

me?" Grinning, he shrugged. "We had a moment behind the bleachers back in high school if I remember right. I didn't want to say anything in case you'd forgotten me."

There's no way I could forget him.

"No, I just…" Her eyes closed for a second. "I didn't recognize you with your cap and shades." Taking a breath, she set her shoulders, reminding herself she was here to do a job, and getting tongue-tied over a guy she'd both had a crush on and managed to sneak a kiss back in high school was *not* a professional look. "Ah, as I was saying, would you like to walk through this house together or are you okay with looking around yourself?"

"I'm sure I want to buy this place, but I'll have a quick look around myself, check out a couple of things." His lopsided smile sent a flood of heat straight through her, the same way it had back in high school. Blushing, Veronica wasn't sure where to look. Swallowing, she managed to gesture to the door ahead of them and mumbled something that sounded vaguely intelligent, and, much to her relief, Chase stepped away.

The second he walked into the kitchen, Veronica dropped her head and let out a slow breath, surprised at the speed her heart was beating.

It's the shock of seeing him, that's all. It's got nothing to do with the fact that he's still a hottie.

"This house is loaded with character."

Blinking back to reality, Veronica lifted her head, clearing her throat. "Uh…yeah, it does."

Come on, I have to get my head in the game. Just because my old high school crush has waltzed into my life again doesn't mean I have to turn back into a giddy teenager.

Steadying herself, Veronica raised her chin and followed him. She had a job to do, and that was the only thing she needed to concentrate on. Her resolve began to slip again when she entered the kitchen and found Chase reaching up to look in one of the top cabinets, his t-shirt lifting a little from the waist of his jeans.

Professional. I am a professional.

All the same, Veronica's eyes couldn't help but linger. Chase wasn't dressing to impress in a blue t-shirt with a faded logo on the front and a pair of well-worn jeans, but all the same, she couldn't seem to take her eyes off him.

"Hmm?"

Veronica jerked and quickly looked away, flushing with embarrassment as she realized Chase had asked her something, and she'd been too busy staring to hear him.

"I asked if you knew much about the previous owner?" Chase lifted one eyebrow, sticking his hands in his pockets as he strolled back towards her. "From the outside – and from what I've seen so far – it looks like this place has been a little neglected and abandoned."

"Yes, it does, but someone was living here," Veronica answered, glad she'd managed to read the file before walking into the house. "An older man with very little family, from what I understand." She took a breath. "I know the house needs some work, and it certainly is a big project, but there are a lot of incredible features here. It would be disappointing to see it torn down."

Chase lifted both arms. "Tear it down?"

"Yes, I thought…." Her face grew hot. "Sorry, I didn't mean to be presumptuous. It's a bit of a trend right now, with companies or individuals buying old houses and knocking them down to build something new."

"And you figured I might do the same?" Chase shook his head, jamming his hands in his pockets.

Hearing the slight edge to his tone, Veronica dropped her gaze. "Like I said, it's on trend right now."

"And those guys are idiots." Chase grinned, taking some

of the bite out of his words. "They don't see the value of things. I wouldn't *dream* of tearing this place down. There are so many beautiful features here that you won't find anywhere else."

Veronica took a deep breath, relieved that the brief tension had faded. "So you plan to restore her to her former glory?"

"Yes, that's my specialty. I've been renovating houses for years now – to the point that I've managed to start up my own company. I have a team who can look around this place and get started the day the sale goes through." Gesturing to the hallway behind her, he smiled. "Let me go have a look at the rest of the house, and I'll be out of your hair."

"There's no rush." Veronica smiled back, reaching out to put one hand on his arm as he walked past, only to pull it away again as her heart began to race. "What I mean is, don't feel you have to hurry. My job is to make sure you've seen everything this house has to offer and that you're happy with it."

"And you're doing a great job," he told her, with a grin that sent sparks into his blue eyes. "I'll take a quick look upstairs and be right back."

Smiling, Veronica nodded and started to turn away, but her eyes snagged on him, watching as Chase walked out to the hallway – and her heart began to beat all over again.

CHAPTER 2

I can't believe Veronica Gillies is showing me around this place.

Chase laughed to himself as he wandered through the upstairs, looking in every room with well-trained eyes, making a mental list of what jobs would need to be done first. He'd recognized her right away, but there was no flash of awareness in her eyes when they'd first said hello.

"She still looks incredible." Chase murmured to himself, his mind back on the moment in high school when he'd taken her hand and snuck behind the bleachers. It had only been a one-time thing but he'd never forgotten it – or her.

Chase tilted his head, glancing at his reflection in an old, dusty mirror. *I wonder if she's with anyone.*

Shaking his head at the reflection, he laughed and turned away. One luxury he didn't have time for was dating. He'd built this business up singlehandedly, and getting distracted when he was taking on a new project wouldn't do him any good.

Although it will still be nice to have her around. Still smiling, he headed back downstairs, happy with everything he'd seen.

Stepping into the kitchen, he saw her before she realized he was nearby. His smile grew. Lost in thought, she rested one hip against the counter, one finger tracing invisible lines on the top, waiting for him to return. From the slight pink in her cheeks, he wondered if she was thinking about what had passed between them back in high school.

I know I am.

He cleared his throat.

"Chase." She smiled, her eyes going to his. "Are you happy with what you've seen?"

The minute he stepped into the kitchen, she was back to business, standing straight, her hands behind her back. "If you have any questions, I'd be more than happy to try and answer them." She waved one hand awkwardly. "I know there are a few odd pieces lying here and there – I think there's a vase in the dining room and a couple of other things like that in some of the rooms, but I'm selling the house and its contents as you see it. So whatever is here, it'll belong to you…or to whoever buys the house."

Grinning, Chase shook his head. "No, I don't think I've got any questions. This place is what I thought it would be. I'm ready to buy it. I like this large kitchen space a lot, although the half wall there is a little unusual."

Veronica glanced over her shoulder. The kitchen was generously sized, but a wall went halfway across the room, almost as though someone had wanted to separate the two rooms but had only gotten the job done partway.

"Yeah, it is a little different, but it does break up the room a little."

"I'd get rid of that." *My head is full of ideas!* "Open it up, make it big and bright." His eyebrows lifted at her. "There is one question you can answer. Is there anyone else interested in the sale?"

Veronica smiled back at him, a tiny smile nudging up

one side of her mouth. "I'm only covering for one of my agents, so I'm only going from the paperwork I've got here." She gestured to the sheets on the counter. "From the looks of things, there is one other interested party, although they haven't come to see the house themselves yet."

"Do you think they will?" Taking a step closer, he let his eyebrows wiggle slightly. "Or if I decide fast, will I get this place before they even have a chance?"

Laughing, Veronica shook her head at him, looking away but still smiling. "Maybe. It depends on how fast you move, I guess."

Chase grinned, his heart rushing at the smile on her face and how it reached up to send light into her eyes. There was an almost imperceptible change between them, but he felt it. The tension at recognizing each other was fading away and being replaced with a rapport he appreciated.

"One thing I do know, though." Veronica bit her lip, her eyes falling to the floor as though uncertain whether to speak. "I'm sure it's nothing, but there have been some rumors about this house. I don't want to dampen your enthusiasm for this project. It's just so you know."

"Rumors?" He hadn't heard of any, but in reality, he had been so busy with the business that he barely had time to eat, never mind take in the local gossip. "What sort of stories are being spread around?"

Veronica's eyes flashed, the slight curl of her lip making him smile. "You sure you want to know?"

"Always good to know the history of a place, I guess."

She laughed. "Maybe I'll regret this. What happens if you don't want to buy it after I tell you?" Closing her eyes, her smile still there, she ran one hand over her forehead. "Wow. This really isn't something any realtor trying to make a sale would say!" Her eyes opened, and she looked away.

Chase smiled patiently. "It's probably because we know each other."

Her green eyes darted towards his. "Maybe."

"And I swear, it won't put me off buying this place." Grinning, he spread his hands out to either side. "You should have seen some of the places I've renovated. I promise it'll take more than a few rumors to get rid of me!"

Veronica blinked, let her lips twist for a second, and, with a smile, shrugged. "Okay, and remember, these are only rumors—" Whether she'd realized it or not, her volume dropped slightly as if she were sharing a secret. "So the man – Mr. Draper – who owned this home before, the one who passed away, there were whispers that his death was suspicious."

Chase frowned. "Wasn't he elderly?"

"Close to it, I think." Veronica shook her head. "I don't know what to make of it, but I know the police were all over this place for a while."

"But they must not have found anything if the house is up for sale now."

Her smile didn't last. "Yes, of course. I was contacted by the estate attorney, who told me that Mr. Draper had specified in the will we were to sell the house and whatever was left inside. It seemed he didn't have anyone to pass the house on to."

Chase grimaced. "Or maybe Mr. Draper knew they wouldn't want it." He glanced around the kitchen. "It's not in too bad condition, but it's sure dated. It's going to need a lot of work to fix it up, but all the same, I think it's worth it." Seeing her watching him, he smiled, lifting one shoulder. "Rumors and all."

"I'm glad to hear that." Veronica released a short breath, relieved the tales had not put him off the house. "Well, it's good for you to know these rumors are going around town right now. You would be filled in by the neighbors anyway, and you might have a few curious onlookers wondering if you'll find anything in the walls!"

Laughing, he saw her cheeks flush and his blood heated. *She's cute when she's embarrassed.* "I'll think of these rumors as a good thing: something that keeps people interested in the house... maybe even enough for one to buy it!"

"Sounds like a good plan." They shared a smile, and before he could stop himself, he blurted out, "Honestly, Veronica, you've not changed a bit. I think I'd have recognized you anywhere. It's so good to see you again."

The rush of red on her face and her soft smile as she dropped her keys told him she was a little embarrassed but grateful for his compliment. "It's great to see you too. I hope this sale works out for you. It is a special property with a lot of potential."

"Oh, don't worry about that." He grinned and folded his arms over his chest again. "I've got every intention of buying this place. I should have the offer terms for you tomorrow. I don't want to waste any time."

"Excellent!" Her face brightened with a happy smile. "I'll look forward to hearing from you."

CHAPTER 3

"*B*ianca?" Veronica glanced over to where one of her employees – and friend – sat. "Can you come to look at this? I want to make sure everything is as it should be."

"You need a second pair of eyes?"

She nodded. "That's exactly it."

The terms from Chase had come through the first thing, and Veronica had been working on it all morning, but another offer had been delivered to her door. "So I was all set with Chase wanting to buy the house, but now I have this additional offer." Shuffling her papers, she found the other buyer's name and pointed to it. "Except there's a problem."

"Which is...?" Bianca looked over the top of her glasses as Veronica's lips settled into a flat line.

Why do there have to be problems now? I want this sale to go through for Chase.

"Okay, so," Pulling up a document on her computer screen, Veronica gestured to it. "Everything is in order here for Chase's offer." Pointing to the accompanying list, she saw Bianca nodding. "I've done the same for this offer from –

Drew Andrews – but it looks like he's missing the proof of funds and the earnest money deposit." She watched as Bianca's gaze flicked down the list. "Have we misplaced anything, do you know? Did anything else arrive today?" Veronica asked.

"The entire package that came through from him is on your desk," she said firmly. "If what you need isn't here, he hasn't sent it."

"Right." Handing the stack of papers to Bianca, Veronica went through them one at a time, and Bianca either nodded or shook her head depending on whether the papers were there. By the time they'd checked it over, Veronica knew she hadn't made a mistake. The documents hadn't been delivered.

"See?" Bianca tapped Drew's name. "You're not wrong. You don't have everything that is required – the proof of funds and earnest money check are missing. Drew Andrews knew what was expected – I was the one who dealt with his inquiry, and I gave him the information document checklist we supply to every buyer. I told him the estate specifically required a cash sale and proof of funds with 10% earnest money to accompany the offer. If he hasn't given you what you need, I'd move forward with the sale to this Chase guy. The attorney asked for a quick sale. He doesn't want a hold up."

Veronica took a breath. "Thanks, Bianca. I appreciate that."

"No problem." Squeezing Veronica's shoulder, she smiled. "Can I get you a coffee?"

Veronica looked up gratefully. "That's exactly what I need. Thank you."

Veronica focused again on the papers. She loved her business. It was what she always wanted to do, but having wonderful agents to work with made the job even better.

And it's nice when the good guy gets the sale.

Veronica smiled, humming as she began to type a few things onto her computer.

I'm glad Chase is getting this house. He's not going to rip it down and build a McMansion like so many other development companies do. I think he's going to turn that place into something special.

Finishing up one document on the computer, she printed out a paper copy and looked it over, only for her gaze to snag on something in the corner of the page. Picking it up, she read it over and closed her eyes with a groan.

"What's wrong?"

Bianca set Veronica's coffee down on her desk, her eyes sharp behind her glasses.

"The police haven't signed off on the investigation, which means I can't get the house sale through until I get an approved copy of *this*." Waving the document around, she sighed and rolled her eyes at no one in particular. "Why is there always so much red tape around these things?"

Bianca chuckled. "You going to call Annie?"

Sighing, Veronica reached for her cell. "Yes. I'm going to call Annie."

It only took a couple of seconds for the call to be answered.

"Hi, Veronica." The warm voice of her friend made Veronica smile. "You know I'm at work, right?"

"I know." Veronica leaned back in her chair. "It's great to have a connection with someone who works down at the station, by the way."

Annie laughed. "Which means you have a question?"

"Yes, I do."

Annie wasn't a cop but an IT specialist at the Excelsior Police Department. She handled video surveillance and wireless communications and had a ton of responsibility. "Okay." The word was drawn out. "What is it?"

"I'm trying to finish up a sale." Veronica glanced at the document again. "It's the late Mr. Draper's house, and I've got a buyer. From what I understand, there was an investigation into the late owner's death, but that has ended. However, there's a document here without a signature, so I can't put the sale through because the investigation hasn't been signed off. Do you think you can help me?"

"It's not actually my job," Annie told her, but Veronica heard the smile in her voice. "But for you, I'll do anything."

Letting out a sigh of relief, Veronica closed her eyes. "Thanks, Annie. I'm grateful."

"Oh, sure. Would you like me to e-mail it over to you once I get it signed?"

"That would be amazing, thank you. It means I can try and get everything finished up by the end of the day."

"Okay, will do." There was a short pause. "You do know there are still all these rumors flying around about that place, don't you?"

"Yeah, I do. I've told Chase about them, too."

"Chase."

"Chase Lawson? We knew him from high school." It was risky talking about him with Annie, who seemed to remember almost everything, but Veronica moved the conversation on as quickly as she could. "He's not bothered by the rumors. Besides, the investigation didn't show anything, did it?"

"No, it didn't." Annie let out a sigh, and Veronica grinned. There was no way Annie was meant to tell her this, but they had such a long and close friendship that their trust in each other couldn't be broken. "From what I can see here, it was ruled accidental. It states they believe he fell down the stairs and, being the age he was — it caused his death."

"That doesn't mean someone wasn't there." Veronica found herself musing aloud. "Maybe they didn't mean for him to die."

Annie snorted, and Veronica could almost feel her eye roll coming across the line. "You planning to change careers and become a cop?"

Veronica laughed. "No, but you know how much I love my mystery novels."

"Maybe too much." There was a smile in Annie's voice, and, used to her friend's teasing ways, Veronica laughed again.

"Yeah, maybe. Thanks, Annie. I'll see you later."

Ending the call, Veronica shuffled through the paperwork to find Chase's number. Typing it into her cell and with a smile still on her face, she waited for him to answer.

"Hello?"

His warm voice made her heart leap, but she kept her mind fixed on the business at hand. *I'm a realtor first. Nothing more.* "Hi, Chase."

"Veronica. I'm hoping you've got good news for me?"

"I sure do." She grinned as he let out a whoop of delight. "The purchase agreement is about to get accepted — once I have one more document I need. I'll message you when it's done. Looks like we can close next Friday."

"That's amazing." The happiness in his voice had her smiling. " I'm so grateful. Thank you."

"Also to let you know." Veronica paused for a moment, and shrugged. "I spoke to someone at the police station. I know now why the rumors are swirling around about the house, but I can promise you that the investigation is over."

There was a short pause. "Okay." Then another hesitation. "Hey, Veronica? Would you be free for a drink after the closing? I'd like to hear what you found out about the house and this investigation. I'm always interested in the houses I buy and their history." He laughed a little too loudly as Veronica snatched in a breath, slightly surprised. "It also might help me understand why the house won't sell if it ever comes to it."

Veronica didn't hesitate for a second. "Sure, I'm free on Friday after work. For a drink, I mean."

"Fantastic. Want to meet at Laurel's? I hear it's a good place for drinks and maybe some food, too?"

Her smile only grew, warmth beginning to push from the swirls in her stomach up to her heart. "Sounds great." Wincing, she closed her eyes, sure she sounded too enthusiastic. "Meet at seven?"

"Perfect. I'll see you then."

"Bye."

An hour after her call, when she'd emailed Chase to let him know the document had come through and the sale was proceeding, Veronica realized she'd been smiling the whole time since their call.

Seems like Chase still has a bit of a hold on me after all.

CHAPTER 4

*C*hase wiped one hand over his sweaty forehead. Okay, so he wasn't thrilled about his appearance right now for his drink with Veronica, but he figured she would understand what he'd been doing all afternoon. He'd gotten the keys only a few hours ago but had been busy. Signing his name on the dotted line, he'd promised to pay a vast amount for a house that he hoped would one day sell to someone who appreciated what it was and what it had become. He'd walked around the house with a pen and notebook, writing down all of his thoughts, all of his instincts as they came up. He needed to know what needed to be removed, what needed to be fixed up, and what needed to be replaced – and he *had* to have it written down instead of using his cell. So far, this two-story house was in pretty good condition, although he was still confused by some marks on the walls.

There were a few pieces of furniture and wall decor left behind – all very eclectic – but behind some of them, he'd found marks on the wall that made no sense. It looked like someone had been drilling and then hastily spackled the holes, although they hadn't done a very good job since he'd been able to spot the marks easily. He crouched low and then stood on tiptoe, looking for any other strange marks, and had ended up a bit of a sweaty mess.

I hope Veronica won't mind.

Frowning to himself, he paused before heading downstairs.

And it's odd that it matters to me how I look.

The thought stole his train of thought as he wandered into the hallway. Inspecting the walls, it was only when a strange, scraping noise caught his attention that he pulled out of his preoccupation and searched around him for the source of the noise.

Taking a few steps he jolted when there was an enormous crash that knocked him back against the wall. At the same time, warmth began to trickle down his forehead.

What just happened?

Blinking, it took him a few seconds to comprehend what he was seeing. He stared at the broken ceramic bust, the ears, nose, and some of its hair now in splinters and chunks on the floor. He glanced up at the ceiling.

"That came from upstairs," Chase murmured to himself, pushing away from the wall and walking to the stairs, squinting up as if someone was going to appear and tell him what had happened. The bust had been one of the odd items left in the house, and he'd left it sitting to the left of the stairs on a small table next to the railing. How had it fallen from the small table to the floor here if he hadn't moved it….

It's not worth thinking about. Old house. Accidents happen.

Something made him blink, and still dazed, Chase put one hand to his temple. Blood dampened his fingertips, and sudden pain from the injury grew like a storm chasing across his forehead. Locating an old rag in the corner of the room, he grabbed it and pressed it hard to his forehead, hoping it would stop the bleeding. The last thing he wanted was to start dripping blood all over the floor.

Speaking of...

He winced. The floor was probably damaged now. He walked back to the marble bust, his steps a little staggered.

It must be the shock.

His lips pulled tight, jaw flexing as he took in the scene for the second time, crouching down to inspect it, one hand pressing the rag to his forehead. He still couldn't understand how it had fallen on him like that. There were no earthquakes. The house hadn't moved, so it had no reason to topple. Besides, he'd thought the railing was higher than the bust itself, which would have kept it back.

No way can I see Veronica tonight.

The stabbing pain in Chase's head grew as he stood up and closed his eyes, waiting for it to fade a little. There was nothing for it. He was going to have to go to the local urgent care center. There was no way he could pretend his injury would be fixed by a band-aid.

Chase headed to the bathroom with heavy feet, gingerly lifting the rag to survey the damage.

Ouch.

There was a three-inch gash across his forehead, and within a second, it was bleeding again. Scowling at his reflection in the mirror, he took in the marble dust in his hair and the blood staining his shirt.

If I didn't look like a mess before, I sure look it now.

Sighing, he pulled out his cell phone, wanting to give Veronica a call before he went. He would have to apologize for not being at Laurel's — maybe tell her he'd had an accident, although he hoped that wouldn't make him sound like an idiot. He hoped she'd understand...and perhaps be willing to reschedule.

A few hours later, he was back at the house, shaking his aching head at the knock on the door.

"You didn't have to come over." Chase pulled the front door open wide. *But I'm glad you did.*

"I know I didn't." Veronica's smile faded as her eyes went straight to his forehead. "You said you'd had an accident? What happened?" She blinked. "I see the hospital took care of you."

He shrugged. "It's nothing." *Plus, the pain meds have really kicked in.* "It was bleeding a lot, but I tried to clean up since I returned."

Ignoring that last part, she narrowed her eyes at him. "I hardly think having stitches in your head is nothing." Dropping her bag on the floor by the door, she stepped closer to him. "What happened?"

Sighing, Chase rubbed at the bandage. "I don't know. I know that sounds strange, but I can't work out what happened." Seeing her frown, he shook his head carefully. "I'm sure you know there are a few things left in the house."

Veronica nodded. "We sold it with its contents, although there wasn't much here to discuss."

"Right." Clearing his throat and aware of how embarrassment was beginning to creep up on him, Chase gestured to the staircase. "One of the items is an old marble bust. It sat on the table at the top of the stairs to the left so I wouldn't run into it when I went up and down. I was planning on bringing it downstairs, but…" Gesturing to the ruins on the floor, he shrugged. "Looks like it made its way down itself."

"That's not funny." Veronica reached her hand up as though she wanted to check his head, only to drop it immediately. "There's blood on your face and your shirt. Are you *sure* you're all right?"

"I'm fine." A little embarrassed, he shrugged. "I didn't have a chance to clean up."

"No need for you to clean up. You didn't know I was going to come over." Veronica smiled at him. Her eyes didn't light up the way they'd done before. "So how would *that* have fallen down all by itself? It doesn't make sense."

Chase took a breath. *No, it doesn't.* "I guess these things happen." He couldn't come up with any other explanation than that. "I think I'll go wash my face, and I'm sure I've got a spare shirt in my bag." He started to turn away, only to spin back toward her. "If you don't mind hanging around here for a few minutes by yourself?"

"Of course not."

Sharing a warm smile, Chase found it difficult to move away. He had to force himself into motion. Moving as quickly as he could, he took a few minutes to clean his face, and the shirt covered in his blood went into the trash. There was no saving it. Thankfully, he *had* brought a spare shirt in his truck, and, while it was crumpled and wrinkled, Chase shrugged it on. It was going to have to do for now.

Wandering back into the kitchen, he studied Veronica appreciatively. She'd found the coffee pot and had poured them both a coffee. "I wasn't sure whether you took cream or sugar."

"Neither." He grinned at her, the ache in his head seeming to fade as she smiled back at him. "I take it black."

"Here you go."

Taking it from her, he thanked her with a slight murmur. "As much as I appreciate this, it isn't the drink I was hoping for."

Veronica flushed, looking down at the tiled floor rather than into his face. "At least we're getting to have one after all." Glancing back at him, she gestured to the kitchen. "Looks like you're getting busy with the renovation already."

When Chase lifted an eyebrow, she waved a hand. "I took

21

a quick look around," she explained. "I hope you don't mind. I do have a question for you, though."

Taking another sip of his coffee, Chase nodded. "Sure. Anything."

"Why have you got all these holes in the walls?" Moving across the kitchen floor to the small dining alcove, she pulled back one of the curtains by the window and bent to study the wall next to it. "Like this. I found it when I went to close up the drapes." Veronica tilted her head back to look at him, her eyes flashing with interest. "I know I made a joke about finding stuff in the walls but I didn't think you'd take it seriously!" Sending him a teasing smile, she straightened. "What are you planning to do? Is it something to do with the wiring?"

"Wiring?" Confused, Chase waited for her to say more but Veronica simply looked back at him, as though he should understand what she was talking about. "Veronica. I haven't put any holes in the wall."

"Really?" Her smile fell slightly. "Well, if you didn't, who did this and the other ones I found too?"

Chase took a breath. "I gotta be honest here, I don't know what you're talking about." He pressed one hand to his head, wondering if he was a little concussed. "Where did you see other holes?" He gestured to the one she had shown him. "This might have been here all along and I didn't notice."

"Oh." Veronica jerked her head towards the stove. "Maybe I'm wrong, but in case I'm not, come on, I'll show you."

Still having no idea what she was talking about, Chase's eyes flared when she pointed to where a large hole was in the wall by the old refrigerator. That *definitely* hadn't been there this morning.

"So you're telling me you didn't do that?" Veronica's voice sounded skeptical. She looked at him in a way that made him worry he suffered from memory loss after his injury.

"No, I didn't." He shook his head and winced, gesturing to his forehead. "I keep forgetting about this."

She smiled sympathetically and reached out to touch the wall, fingers tracing over the hole. "I was sure this had been you." Her eyes darted to his briefly but then back to the wall. "I don't know how else to explain it. This wasn't here when I was doing walk-throughs with prospective buyers. It's new, and if you didn't do it—"

Chase frowned. There was something about this that unsettled him. He couldn't remember putting a hole through the kitchen wall. Maybe he did have a concussion, and he'd forgotten about it. His instincts told him that didn't sound right. He wouldn't have taken a drill to the wall without reason. He'd done plenty of renovations before, and as far as he could see, there was no reason for him to damage a perfectly good wall.

"Maybe we should go look around the house and see if there's anything else."

Veronica's quiet suggestion interrupted his thoughts, and he nodded.

"Good idea. Maybe it's something that neither of us noticed before."

"Maybe." She offered him a brief smile. "I didn't spend much time in this property, so I can't offer much. But I do remember this kitchen."

"That's okay." Taking a breath, he set his shoulders. "That one over there was near to the drapes, right? So let's look behind things, in case they've always been there, and I never noticed."

"Sure." Veronica nodded and headed for the stairs, but as they separated, a prickling sensation overcame Chase, growing stronger with every step he took. Something felt...*off*. He couldn't explain it, but as he searched, the creepy feeling grew even stronger.

There.

His sharp eyes caught another hole in the hallway, which was right down by the front door, hidden away. He might not have noticed it if he hadn't been looking for it, but all the same, there it was. It was the same shape and size as the one in the kitchen and dining room. It looked like someone had drilled a centimeter hole in the wall, but what their reason had been for doing it, Chase couldn't even imagine.

And when did they do it?

The hair on the back of his neck rose.

Someone was in my house, and I wasn't even aware of it.

"I found another one." Veronica's voice echoed down the stairs."I'm in the master bedroom."

Chase swallowed hard, a vision of the statue bust falling from a great height towards him. Fear grabbed at his heart, and before he knew it, he was thundering up the stairs two at a time, desperate to find Veronica to make sure she was safe.

"Veronica?"

When she came out of the bedroom, looking at him with wide eyes, he hunched forward slightly, letting out a slow breath. "Sorry, I was a little…" He closed his eyes. "I think somebody might have been in the house."

Veronica didn't gasp in horror or put a hand to her mouth in shock. Instead, she nodded, as though that had been the exact conclusion she had come to as well.

"It would make sense." Her shoulders lifted and fell. "There's no other reason for these holes, although I don't understand what they're for." Catching his arm, she tugged him back towards the master bedroom. "This was hidden behind an old mirror hanging on the wall. I wouldn't have found it unless I'd gone looking."

Scowling, Chase ran one finger over the wall and the hole within it. It was the same size and shape as the others. "I don't understand why." His hand fell to his side as he turned to face her. "But this is suspicious, and I don't want you getting hurt. You need to be careful."

At this, her eyes widened. "Wait, you think...?" Her fingers curled around his wrist, holding him tight. "You think someone might try and hurt you again?"

"Maybe."

He had to be honest with her, but the second he spoke, her face went sheet white, and she moved a step closer. "Chase, you could have been killed. What if that's what they were trying to do all along?"

"But I wasn't killed," he said firmly, sliding his hand back so her fingers found his instead of grasping his wrist. "I'm fine, Veronica, but there's definitely something going on here. Something I don't understand, and I don't want you mixed up in it. You don't need to be involved."

Tossing her head and clearly ignoring him, Veronica lifted her chin slightly as if to say, *just try and get rid of me.* "First, I think we should call the police."

Smiling a little ruefully, Chase shook his head. "What would I say to them?" His breath came out in a deep sigh. "I've got no evidence. I can tell them what's happened and what I think is going on, but that's not proof—that's suspicion—paranoia. They might log it, but there's nothing they can do."

Scowling, she looked away, her jaw tight. It was like she knew what he'd said made sense but didn't want to accept it. After a moment, her shoulders dropped, and she let out her breath in a hiss. "So, what do we do now? Let this person try and throw something at you again?"

Hesitating, he shrugged. "There's nothing I *can* do." Trying to smile and lighten the mood, he sent her a grin, but it fell flat. "And I guess, from now on, I'll wear a hard hat."

CHAPTER 5

"*Y*ou okay?"

Sighing, Veronica dropped into a chair. "Fine. I had to put up with a guy yelling at me because *he* didn't put in all of his paperwork before the offer deadline, and now he's mad he didn't get the house."

Rolling her eyes, she smiled as Annie handed her a glass of something delicious. "It was sold to Chase Lawson, and this other prospective buyer – Mr. Andrews – seemed to think it was *my* fault he didn't get everything to me on time."

Annie waved a hand. "Forget about him." Her eyes twinkled as she sat back down. "I can't believe you sold that house to Chase Lawson!"

Veronica grinned. "I know, right?"

"I'm assuming he's as gorgeous as ever." Deborah tilted her head, looking at Veronica, who was blushing, with heat rushing up to her face, and she dropped her head.

"I'll take that as a yes." Laughing, Deborah reached across and touched her hand. "I'm teasing, although," she continued with a small smile. "I've heard some things about his little renovation company. They've got a good reputation. He must be hard working and dedicated to what he does to have gotten so much success."

Veronica's flush faded. "I guess so. Looks to me like he knows what he wants and goes for it."

Like he did back in high school.

Her flush returned, and she ducked her head, praying none of her friends would notice.

"They do say a good character is easy to see but hard to find." The fourth of the group, Sarah, smiled gently at Veronica. "I'd say if Chase has come back into your life, fate brought him back for a reason. You have to work out what it is."

"I just sold him a house," Veronica protested weakly, only for Deborah and Annie to look at each other and laugh.

"It's okay if you still like this guy, Veronica. After the way your ex treated you, you deserve someone who's nothing but sweetness."

Veronica rolled her eyes. "We're just friends."

"Friends who spent almost all evening at *his* place?" Annie wiggled her eyebrows. "And here I thought you were going out for a quick drink!"

"I regret telling you all that." Laughing, Veronica shook her head.

The four of them had been friends for years, with Annie and Veronica having gone through high school together. Sarah had moved here a few years ago, and Deborah had arrived only eighteen months ago. They all fit together so well. It was as if they'd known each other forever, telling one another everything that was going on in their lives…. which meant that, of course, Veronica had told them about Chase and his offer of a drink.

"I think if someone called you and said the reason they couldn't meet you for a drink was that they had to go to Urgent Care, you'd want to go check how they were doing."

Her eyes danced from one friend to the next, seeing how they were all grinning back at her. Obviously, Annie had filled the other two in about what had happened between Veronica and Chase back in high school.

"It's okay if you like him, Veronica. You can tell us!"

Laughing again at Sarah's pointed statement, Veronica began to respond, but was interrupted by the buzz of her cell phone. Glancing at it, her smile fell as she grabbed it and saw Chase's message pop up.

Can I call you?

She blinked, a snake constricting in her stomach as she sent him a message back.

Of course. Is there something wrong?

"Is that Chase now?" Annie giggled. "Is he telling you he wants to see you again?"

Taking a breath, Veronica decided to tell her friends the truth. "There's something weird going on at his house." She told them what had happened to Chase and about the holes in the walls, seeing the smiles shatter on every face. "Chase is brushing it off, but I don't think he should."

"So Chase thinks someone else might be trying to hurt him somehow?" Deborah frowned, her eyes darkening. "For what reason?"

"He's not sure." Sighing, Veronica looked at her cell again. Chase still hadn't called. "To me, it feels like someone wants him out of the house, but I don't know why."

Her cell buzzed, and she grabbed it, looking up at her friends for a second. "It's Chase."

"Answer it!" Annie waved one hand. "We'll get out of your way."

"Don't worry about it." Getting to her feet, Veronica hit the green button and pressed her cell to her ear. "Chase. Is everything okay?"

"Yeah." There was a slight hesitation in his tone. "It's

probably nothing, but I wanted you to know I got a weird message today – only a few minutes ago, actually."

A slight frown creased her forehead. "A weird message," she repeated. "What do you mean?"

"I mean the sort of message that's a little…. hostile? It basically said that if I don't put the house back up for sale – the next time, they won't miss."

Veronica closed her eyes, her whole body going rigid. "Someone is threatening you."

"It sure looks like it." His heavy sigh rang through. "I didn't call to frighten you or anything. I wondered if you might be able to help me out?"

"Sure, if I can." *Although I have no idea how.*

Chase let out another breath, and Veronica closed her eyes, trying to keep herself composed. To start panicking now would only make things worse.

"Perhaps you can't do this, but I was wondering if you could tell me the other developers that are here in town? I know some of them do jobs in other places, but it would be good to know everyone who's here right now. I imagine you must have a list?"

Veronica didn't answer him. "You think it's another developer?" In her mind, that didn't sound feasible. "I would be surprised."

"All the same, maybe someone has changed their mind on this place and realized what a goldmine it might be." Chase's voice darkened. "Or it's someone from Mr. Draper's family wanting it back in their possession, but I have no way to find that out."

"So you figured you'd start with the developers."

"Yes. I'm sure this is somebody playing hardball, but I don't go down easily."

Biting her lip at the determination in his voice, Veronica hesitated. *Am I going to do this for him?* "Okay, Chase. I'll do what I can – but please be careful."

"I will."

A sudden idea hit her, and she put her hand to her forehead. "What number did you get the message from?"

"Number? I didn't recognize it. It didn't come up in my contacts or a quick internet search, but I can send it to you if you like, just in case you have it in your contacts." He laughed, but Veronica only winced. Yet again, she seemed to be taking it a lot more seriously than he was.

"Please do."

Chase stopped laughing. "Thanks, Veronica. I...." Pausing, he tried again. "I was wondering if you wanted to stop by the house later. Or we could finally go have that drink?"

"I'd love to come to see how you're getting on with the house." Even though there was a threat to Chase, she didn't let that put her off. "So long as you're not too busy to show me what you've done so far? Maybe I can help!"

"At this rate, you can join the team!"

She blushed, still smiling. "Maybe not quite up to that standard yet."

They shared a chuckle, pulling away some of the tension from the prior part of the conversation. "I'm actually meant to be overseeing things. I've got a team of guys coming in next week to start up the renovations. I'm just doing some things myself. I like to keep busy and make sure I keep my skills honed."

"Oh. Right." Veronica blinked. She hadn't thought about the fact that, so far, Chase was the only one who had ever been in the old house. There was no way one guy could do everything in that place on the timescale he'd mentioned. "Sounds good. I'll come over later. How about I order us a pizza?"

Chase's smile came through his voice. "Now you're speaking my language! I'll see you later, Veronica."

Ending the call, Veronica looked down at the screen, her heart beating faster than expected. Everything in her was screaming a warning about the message, and even though Chase was willing to shrug it off, she wasn't. That threat, in her mind, was real.

"Is everything okay?" Deborah got to her feet, coming over to Veronica as she returned to her seat. "In fact, let me correct that." Her hand squeezed Veronica's arm. "Something has happened. Is it because of Chase? Are you okay?"

Letting out a slow breath, Veronica shook her head. "I'm not okay," she answered, honestly. "There's something weird going on."

She filled them in about the message Chase had gotten. "He's so quick to dismiss it, saying it's probably another developer who realized what they've missed out on, but I'm not sure I believe that – and even if it is, I don't like what they're doing." Smiling briefly at Deborah, she sat back down, appreciating the comfort the chair offered. "He's going to send me the number in case I've got it in my contacts." Her wry smile was matched by the one on Deborah's face.

"I'd say you're right to be cautious." Annie tilted her head, thinking. "I could put it through the database at the station, but he'd have to come to report it first. Do you think he'll do that?"

Veronica bit her lip, then shook her head. "No, not yet, he won't."

"So you're going to put it into your own database?"

The idea made Veronica's heart lurch. "Yeah, that's what I'm going to do. See if it comes up on our contact lists."

Sarah, catching onto the idea, nodded fervently. "That's a great idea, Annie. After all, Veronica, you've worked with almost every other developer in town."

"Apart from Chase."

With a little laugh, Annie shrugged. "It might give you

31

what you need, although I'd still encourage him to take it to the police. That's what they're for."

"Yeah, I know." Letting out a sigh, Veronica passed one hand over her eyes. "I get that I'm taking this more seriously than Chase is, but the whole thing's got me really worried. He could have been killed!"

"And there's no way he's going to put the house back up for sale?"

Veronica shook her head. "No way. He's too determined for that." Swallowing hard, she closed her eyes again as a vision of Chase lying on his hallway floor, blood spilling across it, seared into her mind. "I get that they missed the first time, but what happens if they try again? What if, this time, they don't miss?"

CHAPTER 6

*C*hase looked around the living room, a grin spreading across his face.

This house is going to look great.

A few years ago, it had been a one-man operation, working to fix places, but now, he owned his own company. Everyone he hired was highly trained and worked hard, and the company had gone from Chase doing all of the work from start to finish to a team of professionals he managed – but that didn't mean he was about to sit back and let his skills get rusty. He always worked alongside them, ensuring he picked up any extra slack and helping where he could.

But I always like the first few days with a new place to be me and the house.

Still smiling, he looked up at the ceiling, taking in the period features. Whenever he bought a new place, he always spent time walking through it, getting a feel for it, and noting what he wanted to change and what he wanted to keep. His guys would be arriving in the next day or two, but, unable to help himself, he'd started on some work. Earlier that day and out of sheer interest, he'd pulled back the old carpet on the dining area of the house and, underneath – much to his delight – there had been a beautiful tiled floor. It had been hidden away for who knew how long, but he had every intention of bringing it back to life.

It's going to be incredible. Murmuring to himself, he wandered back through the room, tilting his head as he gazed at the tiled floor. It was dirty and dusty, and there were some cracks and chips and plenty of dirt, but he could envision what it would look like when it was done. The place would be absolutely beautiful.

His cell phone pinged, and he glanced at it before hurrying to the kitchen to grab it, silently praying it wasn't Veronica canceling on him. His heart quietened with relief as the number wasn't one he recognized, only to speed up again when the screen filled with yet another anonymous message.

It's the end of the day. You still haven't called the realtor. Time is ticking.

Something like anger bit hard at him, and he scowled, staring down at the message as though, somehow, if he glared at it long enough, it would disappear. *Which one of these developing companies would do something like this?*

He knew most of the developing firms around here, at least the ones in the state, by name. Some of them were small, like his, and some had big names attached, but he couldn't think of anyone who would do something like this.

Maybe I should respond.

His chin inched up, his jaw jutting forward as he typed.

No, I didn't call the realtor. Not planning to either.

Maybe it was a dumb thing to send, but he wasn't about to let whoever this was start thinking they had the upper hand. He wasn't going to show them an ounce of weakness. People like this were bullies, and he knew only one way to treat bullies.

Gotta stand up to them. No matter how much they threaten me, even if it hurts, I won't give in.

As if the sender knew what he'd been thinking, the screen lit up with a message again.

Then you know the consequences. My patience won't last much longer.

His whole body grew tight with frustration as he sent back another message.

I'm not the type to give up or give in.

Chase shoved one hand through his hair, set the cell phone down on the kitchen counter, and began pacing the room. If it was one of the smaller developers, then that didn't make sense. They were all reasonably close-knit, supporting each other where they could and helping each other to survive. There had been times Chase had let one of his guys work for another company for a short while to help them out. It would be odd for one of them to start threatening him like this.

"Unless something more is going on."

Muttering darkly, he shook his head. He'd told Veronica he didn't scare easily, and that was true, but at the same time, he couldn't help but feel uneasy. Someone had been in his house; someone had thrown something from the top of the stairs in the hope it would knock him flat, and someone had been drilling holes in his walls. He was glad he'd changed the locks today and was sure no one else could get in through any of the windows. He'd ordered a security camera to arrive by the weekend and hoped that would scare off any potential intruders.

His cell buzzed again, and he jerked, startled, only to grab it again. "Hello?"

"Chase?" Veronica's voice was a little hesitant, and Chase closed his eyes, realizing how sharply he'd spoken. *Maybe I'm a bit more jittery than I realized.*

"Hi, Veronica." He tried to smile. "Don't tell me you're the one bailing on our drink this time!" Laughing when she began to protest, he leaned back against the kitchen counter, tension fading away. "Don't worry, I'm only kidding."

"Very funny." She didn't sound like she found it funny at all. "Listen, are you still at the Draper house?"

"Yeah." Chase found himself smiling as he looked down at the floor. He was coming to appreciate Veronica a lot. The sound of her voice had made him smile. "I found a gorgeous old tile floor under the carpet in the dining room. I'm enjoying looking at it."

"That sounds amazing…but if you're not busy, do you think that you could come meet me?"

Chase blinked in surprise. *Does she want me to come over to her place?* "Sure."

"That would be great." Something was hiding in her voice, a slight catch as she spoke, but he couldn't quite make out what it was. "Would you mind coming to the office?"

"The office." *Well, I guess it's not anything close to a date, then.* "It's a little late for work, isn't it?" He tried to chuckle but Veronica didn't join in.

"I have to show you something. I don't want to say anything over the phone, but I think you should come. It's important."

The seriousness of her tone had his smile crumbling. "Oh. Okay, no problem. I think I can be there in about fifteen minutes."

"The sooner the better." There it was again, that slight darkness hidden in her words, and as he promised he'd see her real soon, Chase's stomach dropped to the floor. Why didn't she want to tell him whatever this was on their call?

"Unless…" Remembering how concerned she was, he shoved his cell phone into his pocket and turned around slowly. *Unless she's afraid someone might be listening...or watching.*

Taking a breath, he shook his head. None of this made sense, but he didn't have anything to worry about. Whomever it was – developer or not – they were trying to scare him. Sure, they'd done a good job of almost hitting him with the statue bust, but surely, they wouldn't go further and try and kill him?! That would go too far.

Sunlight had stopped streaming in through the windows as the sky began to darken for the night. Chase shivered as he glanced out of the window and then went in search of his sweater. It wasn't exactly cold out, but he was feeling a little chilled. Whether it was from the call with Veronica or something else, he couldn't say for sure, but he was on edge. Scowling, he grabbed his sweater from the arm of the sofa, slinging it over his arm before he made his way to the front door.

Putting one hand on the handle, he hesitated when a sound caught his attention. He stood still, frozen in place, ears straining for a repeat of the noise. Letting his hand fall, he turned around, ignoring his pounding heart. If there was going to be trouble, then he was ready for it. Whoever was trying to frighten him would find out he'd meant every word he said when he told them he didn't scare easily. He wasn't going to be pushed away from this place, no matter what they tried.

"Hello?" His voice echoed through the house, but there wasn't an answer. Chase rolled his eyes. What exactly had he been expecting? That whoever was here would respond? Pausing, he waited another moment, almost willing the sound to come again, but nothing did.

I must be imagining it.

Grimacing, he turned back to face the door as a creak

came from upstairs. Chase held his breath, closing his eyes to concentrate on the sound.

It came again.

His eyes flew open. How could someone be in the house? He'd gotten new locks and hadn't left any windows open. Had someone come in while he was busy carrying junk in and out of the house?

Frustrated by his own stupidity, Chase took a deep breath, listening carefully. The creak came again, and instinctively, he hurried for the stairs. There was no way he could climb the stairs stealthily – the beams were all too old and creaky. So, with a quick breath of encouragement, he thundered up them as quickly as possible. Rounding the banister at the top, he kept one hand curled into a fist, ready for a confrontation.

There was no one in the hallway.

Chase began to make his way from one room to the next. Pushing open the door to the master bedroom, he strode inside, but it was empty. Moving to the guest bedroom, he did the same – but came up with the same result. It was only when he went into the third bedroom that something exploded from behind him. Too late, he realized, he'd walked into the room without so much as looking behind him, and the intruder had taken advantage. He hadn't hit Chase, hadn't tried to attack him in any way, but had run straight down the stairs and away.

"Stop!"

With a shout, Chase sprinted back down the hallway toward the stairs, but he knew it was too late. By the time he'd hit the bottom of the staircase, the front door was wide open, and there was no sign of the trespasser. Breathing hard, Chase stood on the doorstep, eyes scanning the darkness, but there wasn't a single flash of movement.

What an idiot I am.

Burning with frustration, he rubbed one hand over his face, irritated about how he'd acted without thinking.

"This proves it, though." Murmuring aloud, he headed back to grab his sweater. With his cell phone in his pocket and keys now in his hand, he shook his head, surveying the staircase. "There's something about this house that someone wants."

The question was - what was it they were looking for, and why were they going to such great lengths to get it?

"Veronica."

"In here!"

Turning to locate the muffled voice, Chase pushed through a set of double doors and smiled as his eyes landed on Veronica. She was sitting at a desk to his left, her eyes fixed on the screen and a finger tapping away on the mouse.

She didn't even glance at him.

"This is a great office, Veronica." Chase smiled, trying to push away the rippling tension that still clung to him after what had happened in the house. "You know, you don't have to keep going with this. I appreciate it, of course, but I don't want you to have any trouble."

"Maybe I like trouble." Her green eyes flashed when she glanced over her shoulder, and for a second, she smiled, but then she turned back to the monitor. "Although I think this is more than trouble, Chase. I think this is serious."

A little confused, he came towards her, one hand on the back of her chair as he bent forward, looking at her screen. "What is it?"

"It's this number," Veronica began, clearly ready to start talking about the issue at hand rather than anything else. "*This* is the number that sent you those threats. I've put it into our database, but there's nothing there." She put one hand on his arm for a second. "Nothing at all."

Chase's stomach dropped. "What does that mean?"

Her brow furrowed. "I have the name and the contact details of every developer in the state on my database." She paused for a moment, tilting her head up to him. "Don't you get a Chase? *Everyone.*"

The realization came to him quickly, and something cold trickled down his back. "So you mean to say that none of these people here are involved in what's going on with the Draper house."

"We can't say that definitively." Turning her head back to the screen, she pointed at it. "These guys could have changed their number. Maybe they're using a burner phone."

"A burner phone?" It was hard for him not to keep the wry tone out of his voice. "Really?"

Her eyes narrowed. "You've got to take this seriously, Chase. Please."

Sighing, he nodded, realizing that he hadn't even told her about the intruder in his house. No doubt, when he did, her worries would get even bigger. "I'm trying to," he promised, seeing her shoulders drop slightly. "Another idea for you - maybe it's a new developer? Someone who isn't used to how things work yet? They saw the house and meant to buy it, but the sale went through before they could get everything straightened out on their end."

Veronica shrugged her shoulders. "That could be it." There was a momentary pause. "Or maybe it's something else."

His eyes went straight to hers, seeing how they flickered gently. "What do you think it could be?" He could tell from the intensity of her gaze that she had an idea.

Taking in a deep breath, Veronica set her shoulders. "I think, if it's not a developer, we – *you* – need to maybe call the police."

Letting out a sigh, Chase shook his head. "I don't think we need to. Nothing else happened. I mean, nothing serious."

Veronica blinked. "But something else has happened, Chase, hasn't it?" her eyes narrowed a fraction as he ran a hand over his chin, evading her gaze. "What?"

"It's nothing serious. I didn't get any more stitches in my head."

Again, she put a hand onto his arm, her face paling – perhaps with the memory of his accident. It was the second time she'd done it, and Chase silently admitted he liked the feel of it. It gave him the sense that she cared about him, and that was something he always appreciated.

"What happened?" Her voice was low but urgent. "Why didn't you tell me the second you got here?"

"I didn't want to worry you." Chase sighed quietly. "That's the reason I'm a little late. When I got your call, I was ready to head out, but I heard something."

Veronica's eyes widened. "What was it?"

"Sounds that told me someone was in the house," he told her. "When I heard the noise again, I ran upstairs, sure I would find someone. I opened the master bedroom, the guest bedroom, and then the third guest bedroom and walked into each of them, one after the other." Heat burned its way up his neck and into his face, aware he was going to admit how dumb he'd been. "I just charged into each one and didn't even *think* to look behind the door, and by the time I realized someone was hiding behind the door, they were running down the stairs and out the front door."

The moment he finished speaking, Veronica's eyes closed. She didn't laugh or roll her eyes or tell him that he ought to be more careful. Instead, her fingers slipped down his arm and found his hand.

"I'm so glad you're okay."

He swallowed, feeling her hand on his. "So am I. But next time, I'll definitely look behind the door before I walk into a room."

Veronica took a breath, and Chase lifted his eyebrows at the slight tremble that went through her body.

"Here's the thing, Chase." Pressing her lips together for a second, Veronica looked away, then turned back to him. "My friend Annie - she was in high school with us, but I don't know if you remember her - she works at the Police Department. She's not a cop," she added quickly. "She's an IT specialist. I haven't asked her yet, but she might be able to put this number through their database."

I doubt she'd do that. "I don't think there's any need for that."

"And *I* don't think you're taking this as seriously as you should." Veronica interrupted him, her hand clenching his, her tone rising. "Chase, if you hadn't moved out of the way, that bust would have hit you square on the head. You could have been killed, and whoever did it would have gotten exactly what they wanted."

He blinked.

"This won't go away because you stand up to them." Veronica's voice was quiet, but her words were firm, not holding back for the sake of his feelings. "Words won't do anything, no matter how strong they – or you – are."

Chase nodded slowly, his throat a little tight. He realized he'd been trying to brush it off, telling himself that this would fade away once he'd made it clear he wasn't going to back down. But now, the gravity on Veronica's face told him he wasn't taking it seriously enough, at least not in her eyes.

"They want me to sell, but I won't back down." Standing tall, he let out a slow breath. "So what else is there for them to do?"

His response didn't seem to satisfy her. She shook her head and let out a frustrated sigh, her mouth tugging to one side as she held his gaze.

"You only believe that because of the message they sent

you." A quietness stole over the room as her tone dropped. "What if they weren't meant to miss? What if they're using that as a threat to get what they want, but their real intention was to hit you with that bust? Think about it, Chase. What would have happened if you'd been killed?"

Frowning, he hesitated. "It would belong to the company, and, most likely, they'd put it back up for sale."

"Exactly." She lifted her chin a notch. "So then they'd have gotten what they wanted."

A chill ran over his skin. "If that's true, then why didn't they buy the house when they had the chance?"

In a rather odd response, Veronica caught her breath. Her eyes flew open wide, and her hand left his only to cover her mouth. She blinked, but her eyes remained fixed on his. Chase's heart quickened.

"What is it?" He crouched down so that he could look up into her face instead of looming over her. "Have you remembered something?"

A long breath hissed between her teeth. "Yes." Her face was pale. "Give me a second."

Veronica squeezed her eyes shut, her lashes pressing against her skin as she took in a slow breath. Chase had no idea what she was thinking – couldn't imagine what was going on in her mind, but there was something she had remembered, and it was something significant.

"I'm going to have to ask Annie if she can run this number." Her voice was trembling as she opened her eyes to look straight at him. "But if I'm right, that number is going to belong to Drew Andrews."

The name meant nothing to Chase. "Drew Andrews?"

Veronica nodded. "I think so." She spoke as though she expected him to understand. "I don't know if Annie's going to be willing to do it, but I have to ask."

Chase tipped his head, still looking up into her face, and

realized she hadn't turned towards her computer or cell phone yet. Her face was paper white, her eyes big, and the way her voice trembled meant she was a little afraid. "You don't have to do this, Veronica. You don't have to do *any* of this. I'm not your problem."

Her expression softened, and the edges of her mouth tipped up a little. "That might be true, but I can't forget about you." She shook her head. "I can't forget about *this*." She threw out one hand toward her computer screen. "I've always loved mystery novels, but right now, it feels like we're in the middle of one." Her eyes closed again. "And I'm not sure I like it."

CHAPTER 7

*E*verything inside her was shaking.

I can't believe I missed this.

Chase was looking at her, his eyes roving all over her face, as though by looking, he might uncover a clue as to what she was talking about. Her hand shook as she tried to find her cell phone. "Why didn't I think of this before?"

"You're not making much sense to me, Veronica." Chase pushed himself up to standing as she swung around in her chair to face her computer screen again. "But you sound like you know what you're talking about."

She licked her lips, nervous. "You said something about *why* didn't this person – the one who's been threatening you – buy the house at the time, and it made me remember something. Another person wanted to buy the house at the same time as you, but the sale didn't go through. He didn't get his documents into the office in time, so the house went to you."

Chase caught his breath, his hand going to her shoulder as she tipped her head back to look up into his face.

"Hold on," he said. "You think that the person who's threatening me is the same person who wanted to buy the house at the same time as me?"

Nodding, she put one hand to her throat as it constricted. "Remember I told you there was another interested party? I had to let him know that he hadn't got it, and I got a horrible phone call from him afterward." Her eyes closed as her jaw tightened. "Turns out Drew Andrews isn't the most polite of people. He was aggressive and yelled at me for not letting the sale go through when he was the one who hadn't sent in the proper documentation."

"I didn't know that." Chase's voice had quietened slightly. "I'm sorry you had to deal with that."

"It happens more often than you think." She shrugged her shoulders. "Especially when there's a great house up for sale."

This, for whatever reason, made Chase frown. "But that doesn't explain why he's so determined to buy my house," he murmured as Veronica let her own frown fall low across her forehead. "It's like you said. The Draper house isn't exactly a great buy. It's an old place that needs a lot of work, which is why you believed whoever bought it would tear it down. So why is Drew Andrews so desperate to get his hands on it?"

Veronica closed her eyes. There were too many questions piling on her, too many thoughts swirling in, one after the other. She had to find clarity. She had to make a clear path.

"Okay, first things first." Scouting in a drawer for a notebook, she pulled one out and found a blank page. "Let's try and write out some questions before I give Annie a call. That way, we will have everything clear in our minds."

Chase nodded. "Good idea."

She jotted down the number on the top line, the one that had been sending Chase threatening messages. "We need to know whose number this is. If it *is* Drew's, then he's not using the same number that I have in the system."

"Which would make sense," Chase confirmed with a nod. "He's not going to make it too obvious it's him who's calling, especially if he knows you've got his information on file."

"Right."

Chase's hand settled on her shoulders, and a gentle heat began to worm through her, but Veronica barely noticed. She was too focused on what she was doing.

"We need to consider whether these threats are real or not – and for the record, I think you should be taking them a lot more seriously than you are right now." Turning her head, she arched an eyebrow and sent a steely gaze in his direction, and, much to her relief, he nodded.

"Fair enough." His jaw tightened, and Veronica let out a slow breath.

At least he's realizing how serious this is now. He can't believe he can just send a message back and think that's the end of it.

She took in his clenched jaw and the flash in his eyes and realized he wasn't scared. He was angry.

"If it's *not* a developer who's after this place, then you're right, I need to know who it is and what they want with it."

"So," Veronica continued, writing it down in her notebook. "We need to find out who Drew Andrews actually is. He's not a developer, I know that, but there must be a reason he wants this place."

Chase shook his head. "I don't like this, Veronica. This has got nothing to do with you. You don't need to be involved."

His words softened her heart, and she smiled for a moment. "I can't abandon you and forget about all of this, Chase, after what they did to you." A knife caught the edge of her heart, and she shivered. "I'm sure the police would have ruled your death an accident." She hated speaking like this, but the words kept coming. He had to understand how serious it was. "They would have said that the statue bust falling was bad luck."

Swallowing, Chase looked at her for a long moment, then closed his eyes in thought. "Maybe I should fake my death and see who comes out of the woodwork."

Veronica shuddered, her heart wrenching at the thought. "Don't even think like that. This isn't some bad Sunday night mystery movie."

Sighing, he pressed her shoulder. "Sorry. You're right. I've got to take this seriously as seriously as possible."

"Maybe..." Trailing off, she tapped her pen on her notepad, leaving tiny black ink spots. "Maybe we should tell the police everything."

Chase sighed. "Yeah, I guess so," he agreed reluctantly. "I have the distinct impression they won't be able to do anything but log it, but maybe that's for the best. Maybe them having a record of what's happened is a good thing."

A tiny smile crept across her face. "And maybe we could keep investigating ourselves. If they can't do anything, we can."

Another long breath came from him, but then, he nodded, his blue eyes darkening for a second. "I don't think you'd stop even if I asked you to."

He's right about that.

"But I have to admit, you're pretty good as a detective so far."

She laughed. "I sure don't feel that way. I should have made the connection between Drew Andrews and the house before now. I forgot."

"I don't blame you." Bending a little, he put a hand over hers, his face a little closer now, as his eyes lingered on her own. "You've got nothing to feel guilt for, Veronica. Without you, I don't think I'd be anywhere near where we are right now."

For a second, Veronica forgot about everything. She

forgot about the house, forgot about Drew, forgot about everything else apart from Chase. His hand was warm, and her breath was swirling in her chest. Despite everything else that was going on, she couldn't deny she was drawn to this man.

Then he straightened. His hand lifted from hers, and the moment shattered, leaving her fumbling for a few seconds.

"So," clearing her throat, a little embarrassed, she looked back at her notebook. "I think we need to focus on answering these questions." She tapped on the notebook again. "Find out who Drew Andrews is and if he's still in town, and try to confirm if that number belongs to him.

"One more thing," Chase added, putting one finger on the next blank line of her notebook. "Find out if he had any connection to the late owner."

Veronica nodded. "I'd guess the late Mr. Draper didn't have any beneficiaries." Catching her lip for a second, she thought about that statement, then nodded as if to confirm that the educated guess was a good one. "That's why the house went straight up for sale. If Mr. Draper had a family, surely the house would have gone to them?"

"That sounds reasonable." He ran one hand over his chin. "But that doesn't mean that Drew Andrews didn't know him somehow. Maybe they had a business deal together."

"Maybe," she said.

Chase's lips grew taut, his eyes fixed on the notebook. "But that still doesn't answer the main question."

"What is that?"

"It doesn't tell us what he wants from the house," Chase told her softly. "I still don't understand the holes in the walls. Maybe he's laying traps for me so things will fall apart, and I'll be forced to sell. Maybe he's trying to scare me off somehow, but like I told him, I don't scare easily." His eyes flashed with anger again, and Veronica let out a slow breath. Right now, staring straight into the face of challenge, Chase was proving to her that he didn't have an ounce of weakness and that he wouldn't fall apart. Instead, he was going to force his way forward, stand up against whatever confronted him - and she was just as determined to be there with him.

"Hey, I know it's late, but I brought you some – oh!"

Chase swung around in this chair as Veronica jerked, startled by the interruption. Annie was standing in the doorway, her smile broad, her eyes twinkling as she looked from Chase to Veronica and back again. "Sorry, I didn't know you had company."

"Oh, I don't know if you could call me company." Chase smiled, stuffing his hands in his pockets and shrugging. "Veronica's been helping me out with something."

"I'm sure she has." Annie's voice brimmed with laughter, and heat climbed into Veronica's cheeks.

"Annie, this is Chase. I don't know if you remember each other from high school, but –"

"Chase! Of course." Hurrying forward, Annie stuck out one hand, which Chase shook quickly. "So great to see you again. I hear you bought the old Draper house."

"And I've been having some problems with it," he replied with a grim smile. "Nothing to do with anything Veronica has done, of course."

Annie smiled, sidestepped him, and put a box of donuts on Veronica's desk. "I'll be honest with you, Chase. Veronica told us about the threats you've been getting." Her eyes flickered, her smile faded into seriousness. "I did ask her to tell you that you need to take all this to the police."

"I'm going to." Chase put one hand on his heart as Veronica looked on. "But I figured they couldn't really do anything since there's no real evidence it was all nothing more than an accident... although I did have an intruder today."

Annie's face came alive with interest. "An intruder?"

"Someone was skulking around upstairs. I have no idea what they were doing there. I've also received a few more threatening messages. I'm ignoring them, but..." Spreading his hands, he looked over at Veronica, his eyebrows lifting questioningly as if to say, *We might as well tell her. She works at the station anyway.*

"We're trying to work out who would be trying to scare Chase away from the house." Veronica began to explain as her friend nodded slowly. "I've double-checked the database we have here to see if there's any developer or any buyer who has that number stored in our system."

"But you came up empty?"

Nodding in answer to Annie's question, Veronica sighed and let her shoulders drop. "It's been frustrating, but I do have one name I want to look into."

"Oh?"

Veronica hesitated for a second, hoping Annie wouldn't berate her for doing some sleuthing. "It's a guy by the name of Drew Andrews."

The second she said his name, something flashed in Annie's eyes while, at the same time, she snatched in a breath. Her friend quickly looked away, hoping Veronica hadn't seen it, but it was too late.

"Annie." Veronica's voice was firm, her hand clutching the pen tightly as fierce energy swept through her.

"You know I can't divulge anything." Annie's gaze swept towards Chase. "All I will say is that I would be very careful if I were you."

Veronica licked her lips, seeing Chase's eyebrows drop, sending shadows into his eyes. "So Drew Andrews isn't a pristine citizen, then?"

Hesitating for a second, Annie clamped her lips tight but then couldn't help herself. "Drew Andrews has some convictions."

"So the police are aware of him." Veronica gestured to Chase. "And if he *is* the one behind these threats, then there's an issue."

Annie's hands fastened to her hips. "I get that.

"A *potential* issue," Chase clarified. "We have no proof this 'Drew Andrews' has done anything."

"But he's a likely suspect," Veronica interrupted as, after a second, Annie nodded.

"Again, I'd encourage you to go to the police, Chase. You're right that they might not be able to do anything, but they should still know about it."

Chase nodded. "I'll go by the station tomorrow."

Annie's hands dropped to her sides as she took a long breath. "When I tell you to be careful, it's because Drew Andrews is already known to the police. I don't know much about him; I only saw some of the paperwork going through sometime last year, but from what I understand, he has convictions for burglary and grievous bodily harm."

Veronica sucked in a breath. Chase's eyes flared, but he didn't say anything while her own heart was beating so furiously she was sure it echoed around the room.

Please don't let it be Drew. "Do you think he…?" She took in a deep breath. "Do you think he had anything to do with the late Mr. Draper's death?"

Annie shook her head. "That investigation was closed without anything coming back from it, but, all the same, please be careful – both of you. If Drew is involved, then you need to watch your back. And if he wants that house – or something in that house – then I can guarantee he'll do whatever he needs to get it."

Veronica and Chase exchanged a glance. There wasn't any

trace of fear in his eyes, but the way his jaw worked told her he was thinking hard about how to make sure the house remained his while managing to stay alive at the same time.

"I'll go to the police station first thing tomorrow," he swore as Annie nodded. "But I've got no intention of letting that house go. Drew Andrews will have to learn he doesn't always get what he wants."

CHAPTER 8

"*A*nd that's all you can tell me?"

"Yes. "Chase shrugged. "I know it doesn't sound like a lot to go on, and I don't have any real proof about anything. Don't think for a second I'm expecting you to go and arrest Drew Andrew over this."

"I'm glad you understand." The woman smiled, then dropped her gaze back to the document on the table. She'd taken his statement, and the more he talked, the more Chase realized how little he had. There was no proof yet that Drew Andrews was responsible for anything. Chase had mentioned his name and that he was the one who had wanted to buy the house in the first place but had missed out. He had also talked about the call Drew had put through to Veronica afterward and how she had needed to try and deal with his anger at having lost the house deal, but none of that offered anything significant. It wasn't like the police could turn around and say that yes, it was obvious now that Drew Andrews was the one who had been threatening him and that an arrest would soon be made.

"You did the right thing in coming here." Again, she

smiled at him, but it was only fleeting. "It's good to have all of this logged. I do ask that if you receive any more messages, you will come and let us know immediately."

"I will," he said.

Ever since Drew Andrews' name had been mentioned, Chase had done nothing but ruminate on what it could mean. In his mind, it made more sense to believe Drew Andrews was responsible rather than blame another developer. That notion had never sat well with him, and now he'd had a chance to think about it. He was becoming more and more convinced about the Drew Andrews idea.

Of course, he'd given the police the cell number that had sent him those threats, but the police had only said they would put a trace on it when they could. Unfortunately, it wouldn't take priority. He understood. It was all very vague, and he didn't want to put the blame on someone who didn't deserve it. But all the same, Drew Andrews was the most likely person to him.

Not that my opinion makes much difference to the police.

"Well, if there's anything else, please don't hesitate to get in touch again."

Realizing the interview was over, Chase got to his feet and, with a nod and a word of thanks, walked out of the room and then out of the station. There was nothing else he could say or do, so all that was left for him now was to focus on the house.

It's not like I will give in to these threats anyway.

A wry smile crossed his face as he headed up the street toward the Draper house. It *wasn't* going back up for sale, and he would be carrying on with renovation as planned. He'd changed the locks this morning before he went to the station with the hope that no one else would be able to turn up and walk straight in.

Which means no more strange holes in the wall.

His cell buzzed, and Chase smiled at the sight of Veroni-ca's name on his screen. "Hey."

"Hey." She paused for a second. "So? How did it go?"

"It went well." A little disappointed, he relayed the meet-ing. "But it's as I thought. They can't do anything to help, not really."

"But it's good you went and told them about it," Veronica said as Chase murmured his agreement. "That's all logged. At least *that* is a good thing."

He smiled. "That's true." Taking a deep breath, he let it out slowly again. "So I'm just going to focus on the house and the renovations. My team is arriving in a few days."

"I hope they can just get to work."

"Me too." Shrugging as if he could see her, he smiled. "Maybe me changing the locks is the end of all of this. Maybe whoever it is – whether it's Drew or someone else – has real-ized now I'm not going to back down." With a slight flare of optimism igniting in his heart, he forced a smile. "And it'll all go smoothly, just like I planned."

"I hope it does." There was a short silence. "You know we've never managed to have that drink."

A flash of excitement ran through him, and he had to hold himself back from giving an over-the-top exclamation. It took him a few seconds to compose himself.

"No, we haven't." Relieved at how calm he sounded, he pushed one hand through his hair. "Do you think we'll maybe manage it soon?"

"I was thinking about tonight." There was a short pause. "That is if you're free? And if you…if you want to?"

"I want to."

There had been so much going on with the Draper house, what with the holes in the wall, the injury to his head, and the intruder, Chase hadn't had time to think about his feelings for Veronica. Right now, when she was asking him for a drink, he knew in his heart there was more than just a flicker of interest there. He had liked Veronica back in high school, and she'd blossomed into something even more lovely.

"How about this?" he said. "Since you've been so patient, I'll set everything up at the Draper House." Laughing, he let out a low groan. "I'm going to have to think of a new name for it. I can't keep calling it the 'Draper house.'"

"Maybe the Lawson House?"

"It sounds great, but since I'm planning on selling it, it wouldn't work. Maybe the 'Holey House?'" He grinned at how she laughed. "So what do you say? 8 pm at the house? I'll be able to show you the tiled floor, and I've stuck in an old sofa in the living room for afterward?" Wincing, he let out another groan. "Not sure I'm selling it with that description!"

She laughed. "It sounds great. I can't wait to see the floor."

His heart swelled, sure she wasn't saying it just to try and get his attention. He knew she was interested in what he was doing with the house. Her passion for homes was obvious.

"I think you're going to love it." Enthusiasm warmed his voice. "I'm planning on spending the rest of the day cleaning it and giving it a bit of a polish. It won't be anywhere near done, but it'll look a whole lot better than when I first lifted the carpet!"

"I'm really looking forward to it, Chase. Thanks."

Aware of how his heart had leapt at the warmth in her voice, Chase smiled. "Me too. See you later, Veronica."

Humming, Chase finished up the last bit of the tiled floor. He had done way more than he intended to, but the prospect of Veronica coming gave him an extra burst of energy. Smiling, he rolled up the last few bits of the old carpet and carried it to the front door.

I sure hope she likes it. He glanced at the beat-up table and a couple of chairs. At least they'd be able to sit and eat...

although that meant he'd have to go out and get food. *And I don't want to leave it too late.*

Setting the roll of carpet down, he opened the front door and hefted the carpet over his shoulder, heading for his truck. He could dump the rug and then pick up something for himself and Veronica on the way home.

"That looks like a lot of work." His next-door neighbor smiled at him, leaning on his white picket fence as Chase laughed, falling into easy conversation. They talked for a while, ending with Chase telling him all about the floor and the tiles and how beautiful they were.

The man chuckled. "Well, you're doing a great job. It takes a special type of person to take on a place like this!" He was an older fellow with a heavily lined forehead, an easy smile, and bright blue eyes. "I gotta say, Mr. Draper was a very quiet sort. He didn't have anyone coming round much, only his nephew."

Chase smiled sadly. "That's sad."

His neighbor rolled his eyes. "I don't think Mr. Draper wanted his nephew here. Whenever he came around, they were always yelling and fighting. I'll be glad not to have that any longer!"

A sudden thought struck Chase. "You say this was his nephew? I thought I heard he didn't have any beneficiaries." He waved one hand to the house. "The house was sold just as it was seen – not that there was much in it." Seeing the man's frown, he explained. "Just an old bed in the master bedroom, a few ornaments here and there, and a single chair in the living room."

"That sounds like Mr. Draper." The man shrugged. "Frugal to the point of being broke. I think that's why that place is still run down. He never put any money into it."

"It's hard to do if you don't have a lot of spare money rolling around." Glancing at the rolled-up carpet, Chase grinned. "Speaking of rolling, I'd better get that carpet to the dump. It was great to talk to you."

The man smiled and headed back into the house, leaving Chase to do the same. He'd need to grab his cell and his keys before he left. A curl of excitement rose in his chest as he thought about meeting Veronica, only to frown and shake his head to clear that thought away.

"Just a drink, Chase. It's just a drink." Murmuring to himself, he walked into the kitchen just as his cell buzzed. Grabbing it, a frown formed across his forehead as he read the two short words.

Time's up.

That was all it said. Ignoring the slight stab of worry, Chase rolled his eyes, ignoring the threat. *I'll have to let the police know. I said I would.*

Taking a screenshot of it, he deleted the message without even thinking about replying. He'd made himself quite clear in his previous messages. He wasn't about to be intimidated, which meant ignoring every message from whoever this was. Part of him was tempted to message back, telling Drew – if it *was* Drew – that he knew who he was and that the police knew too...but Chase resisted. He shared everything with the police, and he would let them do their job. That number would be traced, and hopefully, he'd find an answer as to who was threatening to take this house from him.

Tilting his head, he paused for a moment. *I don't even know what they're looking for.*

Frowning, he dropped his cell on the kitchen counter and wandered to the window, finding the hole in the wall that Veronica had discovered the first time she'd come over. Bending down to look at it again, he let his fingers run over it, his lips twisting. Why would someone drill holes in the wall like this?

He blinked. *If I had a small enough flashlight, I could see in here.*

He thought about that for a while, only to shake his head. It would have to be a strong flashlight and a *really* small one at that... although maybe someone had an extendable one, one that could push forward and shift through the space between the walls. Now that he thought about it, couldn't you get those mini-extendable cameras these days? That sort of thing would be able to fit through the hole in the wall and record what was in the space.

"You were right all along, Veronica." He said out loud.

It seemed like someone was looking for something in the wall, after all. The walls weren't thick, but then again, someone could hide something fairly small between them. What that something could be, though, he had no idea.

Although maybe tonight we can keep the mystery talk to a minimum.

It would be nice to talk to Veronica about all things Veronica. They could discuss hobbies, life, and what she'd been doing since high school. He could tell her about his company and how things were going, and how much he'd enjoyed getting to know her again.

And I always told myself I was too busy to date. Turns out I was just too busy to date anyone apart from Veronica.

Laughing softly, he ran one hand over his eyes before getting to his feet and heading into the hallway.

So long as she wants to date me, too. I haven't even asked her yet!

Before he could think another thought or make a single sound, something hit him so hard that he staggered forward, dazed. It paralyzed him. He couldn't even speak, couldn't even shout, as the pain began to blind him.

The last thing he was aware of was falling into the waiting darkness.

CHAPTER 9

*S*omething's wrong.

Veronica glanced at her cell. She'd called Chase about six times, but he still hadn't picked up. She was running late. A sale had snagged a hitch, and she'd needed to stay and help Bianca so they could get it through before the weekend. She'd tried to call to ask him to wait, but there was no reply, and now, the longer she waited, the more anxious she grew, sure that he would be expecting her but wondering why he wasn't answering his cell.

"Is that it?" Leaning forward, Veronica put her hand flat on the desk and gazed at the computer, her other hand curling into a fist and desperately waiting for the title company to say, yes, we have the clear to close. That was all that was needed, and why it had taken so long, she couldn't understand. Technology has a way of making the most straightforward things all the more difficult sometimes.

"Yes, that's it." Bianca turned to her with a smile. "Thank you. I'm so glad that went through. I think we would have had problems tomorrow if it hadn't."

Veronica managed to smile. "Sure, no problem, Bianca.

Sometimes these things happen, and technology lets us down." Her eyes went to her cell again, but there was still no message from Chase, no flash on her screen to let her know he was calling.

Following her eyes, Bianca lifted an eyebrow when Veronica looked back at her. "Something wrong?"

"I was – I'm supposed to meet up with Chase." She shook her head. "We are having drinks together at eight o'clock."

"But it's nine now." Bianca's face flushed, her eyes widening. "Oh, you should have said you had another engagement. This could have waited."

Veronica shook her head. "No, it couldn't have. You and I both know how important this is. That's not what bothers me. I'm concerned about the fact that he hasn't called me back. I thought he would have been wondering where I was by now. I've called him six times, and he still hasn't picked up."

"That is a little odd." Bianca made a shooing motion with her hands. "But there's no need for you to stay around here. Get going! I'm sure he'll be waiting for you. Maybe he's left his cell behind somewhere and doesn't know where you are, so he's just standing, waiting until you turn up."

Veronica convinced herself that it was the most sensible explanation. "Thanks, Bianca." Giving herself a small shake, Veronica went to pick up her bag. "There's just this weird thing with the house and another guy who wanted to buy it – Drew Andrews." She shrugged. "Chase has been getting threats, and I'm so sure it's from Drew, but we can't be sure. Nothing's come up in our system, and the police are trying to trace the number now, but they haven't called with anything yet…. at least not as far as I know."

"That Drew Andrews is a nasty piece of work." Bianca folded her arms and sat back in her chair, her eyes glinting behind her glasses. "Just as well he didn't get the house. You need to steer clear of him. His uncle didn't like him, and neither does half this town."

Veronica's heart stopped dead. "His uncle?"

She saw Bianca's eyebrows lift as though she had expected Veronica to know whom she was talking about. "Yes, his uncle was Mr. Draper," Bianca spoke slowly, ensuring Veronica could take everything in. "As I said, they didn't like each other very much. From what I know, there's not much to like about Drew Andrews, anyway."

Turning, she typed something on her computer, and her screen showed a photo of a tall, broad-shouldered, blonde-haired man who wasn't smiling. "This is him. He was probably furious when his uncle cut him out with the will. I believe Drew is the only living relative, so I guess he expected to get everything."

It was like all the air had been sucked out of the room. Veronica couldn't even take in a gasp of breath as she stared at her friend with wide eyes. A slight pounding sounded inside her ears as she absorbed what Bianca had just told her.

"Veronica, are you okay?" Bianca got up, one hand going to Veronica's arm. "You've turned a very odd color."

"I – I didn't realize. This means that…"

Trailing off, Veronica drew in a ragged breath and closed her eyes, feeling like a hand was squeezing her throat. It took her a few minutes to find enough composure to speak. "I didn't realize he was related to Mr. Draper. They have different last names, so I didn't even think."

"He's the son of his sister." Bianca's hand waved at the screen. "Although there's not much of a family resemblance. Sorry, Veronica, I thought you knew."

Veronica managed a small smile, still blinking. "And I should have asked you. You know almost everyone and everything that goes on in this town." Another deep breath helped her to calm down a little more. "This carries a lot of weight, Bianca. It means there's a connection between Mr. Draper and Drew Andrews that we didn't know about before. And I'm guessing the police don't know much about it either. Annie would have mentioned it otherwise."

Her friend nodded. "Drew Andrews doesn't always hang around town either. He was always going off traveling somewhere, but now and again, he'd come back to see his uncle. I used to think it was sweet until his neighbor, Mr. Jones, told me about the blazing arguments they used to have at all hours of the night!" Sighing, she rolled her eyes. "I could never understand why Drew Andrews kept coming back to this place if he hated his uncle so much."

Because he wanted something.

Veronica blinked furiously and forced air into tight, strained lungs as her mind flooded.

And he didn't get it before his uncle died...which means he will do whatever he has to. Chase is in his way, but Drew will get rid of him, one way or the other.

It felt as though she'd forgotten how to breathe. Only when Bianca touched her arm again did she realize she'd been staring ahead.

"And he's got a criminal record," she whispered as Bianca's eyes flared. "Annie mentioned it to me. She knew his name and told me to be careful. He's been convicted of theft and grievous bodily harm." Her whole body shuddered as she pictured Chase alone in the house, unaware that Drew Andrews was not only coming to get him but was determined to get whatever he wanted in whatever manner he needed. "I've got to go and tell him! I've got to warn him."

"You want me to call the police?"

Veronica shook her head. "No. Not yet. Chase might be doing just fine. He might have left his cell phone, just like you suggested." *Which means calling the police would do nothing but embarrass us both.* "I'll call them myself if I need to."

"Okay." Bianca's voice echoed down the hallway as Veronica ran to the door. "Be careful!"

Standing at the ajar front door of the old Draper house, Veronica let her eyes rove over every dark shape, telling herself she wouldn't be afraid.

"Chase?"

Whipping out her cell, she enabled the flashlight function and crept in, ignoring the screaming that came from her mind, cautioning her to run away. The open front door had her worried, but with the whole house in darkness, her instinct that something wasn't right fired like crazy.

So where is Chase?

Thoughts flew through her, blood roaring in her ears as she took one small step after the other.

What has Drew done to him?

Drew was the sort of man who made threats and kept them, and that meant, since Chase hadn't put the house up for sale, the worst was going to happen. A sob caught her throat as she blinked tears away from her eyes.

I pray I got here in time.

"Chase?" Her voice echoed around the hallway as she called his name as quietly as possible, worried someone else was in the house. Her heart was beating so hard it was painful, her stomach clenching, twisting, and rising as she moved forward into the house. She half expected a hand to grab her wrist at any second.

Although if he comes out of the bathroom or something and sees me creeping in like this, I will feel like such an idiot.

"Chase?"

Her flashlight lit up a dark, shadowy place by the stairs, and Veronica stopped suddenly, one hand flying to her mouth, the other beginning to shake as she fought to hold her cell up. A deep and dreadful fear began to wind around her as she fought to breathe. Chase was lying on the ground beside the stairs. He was face-first on the floor, and she was sure the darkness on the back of his head was blood.

Her stomach lurched, and, for a moment, she thought she might be sick, stumbling back and falling against the wall, leaning against it for support. Her eyes were fixed on him, her breathing coming in ragged gasps. She couldn't seem to tear her gaze away, afraid now that the man she was looking at, the man she cared about, was dead.

Am I too late?

Closing her eyes to shut out the sight, Veronica steeled herself.

I have to find out. I can't just leave him lying there.

Before she could move, a sudden sound came from the back of the house. Veronica froze, her skin prickling with fear. Her eyes went to Chase, praying he would give her some sign of life. She couldn't seem to move, still pressed hard against the wall, hands splayed, legs shaking.

They might see the flashlight.

Shutting it off, she slid the cell phone back into her pocket, trying to calm her raging fears.

Another shout came from the same place, and it got a reply this time. Whomever these people were, they were somewhere in the back of the house and soon might move to the front — to her and Chase.

Drew. It has to be Drew.

Veronica knew in her gut that Drew Andrews was behind all of this. She didn't understand why he was doing this, didn't know his reasons, but she was sure he was the one going after Chase, threatening him, demanding he sell, and now injuring him.

Chase groaned.

Veronica's eyes widened, her stomach knotting as she gritted her teeth and peeled herself away from the wall. Nobody had thundered into the hallway yet. No one, it seemed, had heard her enter the house. No one had seen her yet, which meant she still had time. She had to get to Chase and try and save him before they came to do something worse to him.

"Chase?" She crept towards him, her legs shaking. She prayed the floorboards wouldn't creak as she bent down beside him. "Chase, are you okay? Can you hear me?" Leaning forward, she touched his shoulder, keeping her eyes away from the blood. *"Please* say you're okay. Wake up, Chase, please! I need you to wake up."

CHAPTER 10

Someone was calling his name. He had no idea who it was and couldn't understand why his eyes refused to open. They were heavy, sinking down into his skull, refusing to do as he asked of them.

"Wake up, Chase, please. I need you to wake up."

Something touched his cheek, a gentle hand brushing his skin. He tried to speak, wanted to say he was awake, that he would get up in a minute and, whoever this was, needed to stop needling him, only to realize that he wasn't in his bed. Something had broken through the unconscious state he'd been in, and now, his mind and body were trying to rouse themselves again.

"Umph."

It was the only sound he could manage. His eyes were still closed, but he demanded they move, every bit of strength going into such a simple action. He heard a half sob, half cry of relief, and realized Veronica was beside him.

"Are you okay?"

Chase drew in a breath, pain coming to him like a crashing wave. His whole body seemed to burn with it, and it took him a few seconds to answer. "Where am I?" His throat was tight. "What happened?"

His graveled voice seemed far too loud for his ears, and he dropped his eyes closed again, shutting out the blurry vision of Veronica. The pain in his head was immense. He couldn't remember what happened. The only thing he could think or feel was pain.

"I'm so sorry, Chase." Veronica's voice was a whisper, but it was like a trumpet blast to him. "I know this sounds awful. You need an ambulance, but you have to get up. We have to move. We can't stay here."

Chase tried to say something, but the pain only intensified. Veronica had one arm around his shoulders, the other one at his chest as she murmured words of encouragement. He didn't understand why she was whispering, but he forced himself to do what she wanted, his whole body shaking with the effort.

This isn't me.

Being weak wasn't a sensation he was used to or liked. He never pulled back from anything and was never held back by any threat or obstacle. Chase gritted his teeth, hating the weakness that burned through him now. Scowling hard, he set his jaw and, with Veronica's help, managed to push himself to his knees.

"What... What happened?"

It took a few seconds for the dizziness to fade, but as he spoke, his vision cleared until he finally saw Veronica clearly. Her eyes were huge.

"I don't understand." He said, reading her face.

A sound seemed to come from far away, and Veronica clapped one hand to her mouth, her eyes flaring, and he realized in that instant just how much trouble he was in.

It's no accident that I'm in serious pain and lying on the hallway floor.

"Someone else is here in your house," she whispered.

Chase rubbed his eyes, the realization sending a wave of strength into him. "Someone's in my house. They did this to me?"

"I guess so. We have to go. We can call the police from outside." Veronica took his arm and helped him to his feet, her voice still not much louder than a whisper. "Whoever is here, one of them attacked you so you'd stay out of their way. And I don't think they'll stop until they get what they want from this house." Her words ended in a squeak as low voices grew closer to them. "We don't have time to get out the door. Come with me!"

Chase didn't have much choice, still leaning on her as she turned into the living room. It was all becoming clearer, but it was taking time for his mind to stop being fuzzy. The agony of the injury to his head was overwhelming. He couldn't draw breath without pain, but, at the same time, the instinct in him to protect Veronica grew. If only his body weren't so heavy and sore, then maybe he would be able to do a little more.

"Down here."

The old sofa he'd brought into the house — the one where he or his men could sit whenever they needed to break — was a perfect place to hide behind. Okay, so it wouldn't do much since someone could just poke their head over the top and see them — but it was better than nothing. Plus, it was dark.

Sinking down to the floor, Chase let out a long breath and rested his head against the fabric, only to let out a yelp.

"Shhh!" Veronica's eyes flared. "We left the door open, and whoever was at the back of the house is in the next room."

Chase swallowed. "I'm sorry." His eyes closed tight again. "I shouldn't have gotten you into this."

Veronica's eyes were still big but fixed themselves on his. "You didn't do anything. I made myself a part of this, and I'm sure glad I did because who knows…." Her eyes closed tight, and she turned her head away, her lips trembling. "I don't know what they did to you, but I'm sure glad you're okay." Her voice softened even more. "We *need* to call the police."

Her hand went to her pocket as Chase looked on, only for her to freeze. Her head dropped, her hands going from one pocket to the next, patting them desperately.

"What's wrong?"

"I – I don't know where my phone is. I had it when I came in, but it must have fallen out of my pocket when I went to help you."

Nodding slowly, Chase tried to think about what they could do next, his hand reaching out to touch her fingers. "I left my phone in the kitchen." Grimacing, he closed his eyes again. "I don't remember much else apart from walking into the hallway and something hitting me… twice."

Her fingers curled around his. "Like I said, we need to get you to the hospital."

"Don't think that's going to be possible," he murmured.

Hearing voices and what sounded like drilling coming from the hallway, he shook his head. "I think they're in the kitchen. Which means we'll be seen if we go out that way."

"Can we get out the window?"

He shook his head. "They're jammed shut." Shrugging, he sighed. "An old house has a lot of problems, and that's one of them. I didn't think it was a priority." Squeezing her fingers, he managed a wry smile. "Looks like you were right about all of this, Veronica. It was much more serious than I ever imagined."

"I *hate* that I was right." Her lips thinned. "That doesn't help us a lot. What are we going to do now, though? Any ideas?" Her eyes searched his face. "Are you going to be okay to walk?"

He nodded and kept his expression blank even though pain shot through him again. "I'll be fine. Okay, so whoever these guys are, they want something in this house. It looks like they're not going to stand around and let anyone get in their way, which includes me." A jolt of fear had him gripping her hand hard. "And you."

There was broken laughter from their unwanted visitors and Chase closed his eyes, trying to think. "And I'm sure someone is going to notice that I've moved."

"You were lying in the shadows right beside the stairs." Veronica pursed her lips for a second. "They're distracted enough not to notice…. right now, at least." Her voice was barely audible, but the flash of concern in her eyes was unmistakable. "Chase? I know who this is."

Chase blinked. "Are you sure?"

Veronica nodded, her gaze steady. In fact, she seemed calmer and more collected than he was. He was so grateful for her, he realized. Thankful that she'd shown up, thankful she'd come to look for him. He didn't want to imagine what would have happened if she hadn't. "Who is it?"

Voices grew closer to them, perhaps two men stepping out from the kitchen into the hallway. From the gap in the door, they could overhear something about sledgehammers, and from the way Veronica's face paled, Chase imagined he wasn't the only one thinking about what they might be using those sledgehammers for.

They're quieter than a gun.

"It's Drew Andrews." Veronica's voice had a slight tremble, but determination flickered in her eyes.

"Are you sure?"

The voices faded, and Veronica nodded, swallowing hard. "Absolutely. I never made the connection because they have different last names, but Bianca told me Drew Andrews was the nephew of the late Mr. Draper."

Surprise stole his breath for a second. "What?"

"I know. Mr. Draper's will stated that this house was to go up for sale, and that made Drew real angry." She shook her head. "Angry enough to do whatever he had to if it meant getting this place back." Her hand went to his arm again. "You changed the locks. Any idea how he – or one of his guys – got in?"

Nothing came to mind, only for something to slam back at him, burning shame into his mind.

"Oh no." He dropped his head, rubbing one hand over his eyes. "This afternoon." *I left the front door open when I went to take the carpet to the truck.* "I had to take an old carpet to the truck so I could go to the dump, but instead, I ended up talking with the man who lives next door."

"Mr. Jones?" Veronica managed a slight smile as her eyebrows lifted. "He's friends with Bianca. She was the one who told me about him."

"Right." Taking a breath, Chase continued, a little taken aback by how much Veronica had managed to find out. "He told me that this guy, Mr. Draper, had a nephew who used to come around. He said they argued a lot." His eyes closed for a second. "He said there were a lot of arguments, banging and shouting and things like that. I never knew it was Drew Andrews."

It's so strange how someone I've never met is causing me so much trouble.

"And you think he wants something in this house?" Chase asked.

"It's got to be," Veronica murmured. "First, I thought he just really wanted the house – I mean, I'm sure he does – but now I think he wants something *in* it. Since he can't legally get it unless you sell it, the only way to try and do that is to threaten you, to force your hand so you do what he wants. And if you don't do it, then...."

"Then I'm going to get hurt, and he'll come for what he wants anyway," Chase finished, his eyes closing tight. "Yeah, he did a pretty good job of that." As he turned his head, shifting his body a little to look at her straight on, the pain rose to a crescendo, but he fought his way through it. "We need to get out of here."

"But if we don't have our phones, how will we call the police?"

"I guess that's the first thing we have to do." Chase took in a deep breath, forming a vague plan in his mind, as Veronica looked back at him, waiting for him to add more. "We need to find either your cell or mine. Then, I need to go out and call the police." His jaw worked for a second. "You can get to your car. I want *you* to be safe."

Veronica's eyes flashed, her chin lifting. "I see what you're saying, Chase, but I can't let you. You can't stay here until the police show up!"

"I *have* to." Chase took a deep breath. "I have to be able to see Drew Andrews. I have to see his face. If I don't, then he could slip away, and no one will ever know he was here."

She shook her head. "It's too dangerous, Chase. It's not worth the risk."

"I think it is." Glancing down at their joined hands, he took a steadying breath, setting his shoulders as best he could. "I have to have the proof he was here, that he was behind this. If I don't see him in my house, then it's only my word. That won't hold any water, and he could get away with everything. And, no doubt, start over."

He heard her catch her breath.

"I have to do this, Veronica."

"Then I'm staying."

Chase caught her gaze at once. "You can't!"

"I am." Her expression was calm but determined, glints of steel in her eyes. "I'm not leaving either, not until we've both seen him here. Plus, you've got a bit of a problem with your plan."

Frowning, he looked at her. "What?"

"You don't even know what he looks like. It sounds like there are a few guys in the other room and you won't know who is who – or if Drew is even there!" Her lips flattened, waiting for him to argue, but Chase said nothing. He didn't have an answer.

"*I* know what he looks like," she finished, squeezing his fingers. "I saw his photo before I left the office. So it looks like I'll be staying right beside you whether you like it or not."

Despite the situation, despite the pain in his head, he couldn't help but smile. "You really are incredible, Veronica." Her smile, even in these circumstances, was warm. "When we get out of this, I swear we're going for that drink."

Her smile grew. "We've never managed to get that so far, have we?"

"Nope." Light humor took away the seriousness of their situation for a few seconds, giving Chase time to gather the strength to work through what would happen next. "But once we get out of this, that's what we'll do, right? It doesn't matter the day, it doesn't matter the time, we'll go out and get that drink, just like we always planned to."

"Sounds great to me."

He nodded and looked towards the kitchen. "Okay, I'm going to go to the door. See if I can work out what's going on."

"I'll come with you. I –"

"No." He lifted her hand, kissed the back of it, and cut her off gently. "They don't know you're here yet. They think it's only me. If I get caught, you have to get out of here as fast as you can…somehow. If you can't find your phone, go to the neighbor and get him to call the cops, okay?"

He thought she was going to argue for a second, but then her jaw set, and she nodded, looking away from him. "Okay." Her eyes flashed at his. "Pity you never got around to fixing up those windows."

Chase got to his feet with a small smile, trying to ignore how his head exploded with pain. The next second, however, Veronica grabbed his hand and tugged him back down just as the sound of a crash rang out through the crack in the door.

Someone began to cough, and there were shouts and a whoop of evident excitement. The smell of dust and broken plaster began to make its way through the edges of the living room door. Chase stared back at Veronica with wide eyes, the shock he felt mirrored on her face.

"What on earth was that?"

CHAPTER 11

*V*eronica stared at Chase, her heart heaving behind her ribs. She had no clue what that sound could have been, and from the way Chase's eyes rounded, it was apparent he didn't know either.

"Are they tearing down the house?"

Chase looked away. "Whatever they're doing, we need to move. Maybe seeing Drew's face isn't as important as I thought."

Swallowing against the tightness in her throat, Veronica leaned closer to him. "As much as I hate this, I agree with your original plan. One of us has to see him here – and be able to state on record that we know he was in the house. If we don't, then he could come after you again – maybe not him personally, but I'm sure he'd be able to hire someone to finish the job he started."

Chase blinked. "And if the police show up, he'll be out of here before they can catch him." Taking a breath, he leaned his head against the back of the sofa again.

Veronica nodded, thinking hard. "They're busy concentrating on whatever they just destroyed – whatever that crash was. We need to use that diversion to go and get my cell. That's the first thing."

Scowling, Chase closed his eyes for a second. "I don't like it."

"I know, but what choice do we have?" Her determination was steady, and when he frowned, she offered him a shrug. "You're a mess, and I need to get my cell phone. Plus," she added with a small smile. "It's not as though you're in any state to sneak out to get it! The only place you should be right now is a hospital – and I need to get you there as soon as possible. Once I get my cell, I can call the police and ask them to come in quietly. That way, we're both safe." *Or as safe as we can be.*

"Okay." With a quick nod, Chase got to his feet. Seeing him wince, she paused but stepped away, hearing him follow her.

Careful, Veronica. Don't make a sound.

She planted her feet, relieved that Chase could walk without her help. When he stepped closer to look through the gap in the door, she gasped at the trickles of blood running from his head down the back of his neck.

After a few seconds, he turned away. "I can't see much of anything. There's a ton of dust clouding the air, but I have no idea where it's coming from."

"It can't have been in the hallway," she said, following his gaze. "We'd have seen the plaster on the floor."

Chase's eyes widened. "There's that half wall in the kitchen, the one that separates the kitchen and the dining area."

Her heart leapt. "You think they're looking in there?"

"I think they've knocked it down," he answered grimly. "I still don't know why, but that's my guess."

"Well, this is our only chance. With that dust cloud hiding me, I can slip out and see if I can find my cell. It must be near to where you were." Veronica stepped forward, but Chase turned, one hand on the edge of the door as if he wanted to stand between her and the hallway.

"You can't, Veronica. It's too dangerous."

He's trying to protect me. "I have to."

"What if someone sees you?" Swallowing, he gestured to the windows. "We can try and get you out another way – or if they're as distracted as we hope they are, then just go for the front door. Run. Go and find anyone you can." His hands fell to his sides. "I can't run, not like this. I'd end up getting us both..." Trailing off, he closed his eyes, not wanting to end the sentence but reminding her of the risks, nonetheless.

Veronica bit her lip. As much as she understood what he was saying, she was determined not to leave him. She had to see this through.

"No way I'm leaving you here *or* running away and risking you being found out because of me." Her hand found his. "Let me go get my cell. As I said, we can call for help after that."

A long sigh came from him, but eventually, he nodded.

Then I gotta go.

"Thanks, Chase."

"Okay." From the sound of his voice and the way his eyes flickered, Veronica knew he wasn't happy about it – but what other choice did they have? When she moved to slip through the door, he held her shoulder for a second. "Please be careful and be as quick... and as silent as you can."

"I will."

Her nerves were jangling, a slight tremble running over her skin, but she didn't hesitate. Pressing herself against the wall, she slipped down it carefully, trying to stifle her furiously beating heart. She heard the sound of voices from the kitchen.

I need to get my cell.

She forced her gaze back to the floor where she'd originally found Chase. Moving stealthily, she scrabbled around in the shadows, praying she'd be able to find it.

My heart's beating so loudly, I doubt I'd hear Chase even if he shouted my name right now.

Much to her relief, something flashed and reaching for it, her fingers clasped around the familiar shape of her cell. Holding it close to her chest, Veronica pushed herself up against the stairs...only to pause and hold her breath.

Now's my chance. If I'm brave enough, I might be able to see who is here and what they're doing.

Courage had never been something she'd needed a lot of before, but right now, Veronica needed it in bucket loads. Ignoring Chase's whispers, she slid toward the end of the staircase, peering toward the kitchen. The shadows still clung to her, but the dust was settling, and as she moved forward even more, Veronica became aware of the growing light reaching out for her.

Gotta be careful.

Her eyes went to the crack in the door, widening as she took in the scene.

Chase is right. There is a lot of dust here. They've definitely knocked something down.

Her eyes narrowed as she focused on the kitchen. She couldn't see much, but from what she could hear, the men were in there. Something was buzzing, like a drill, and the occasional thump from something falling on the floor. Someone laughed, and Veronica jerked back, her stomach twisting.

"What are you doing?"

Turning her head, she saw Chase beckoning her from the shadows. She held up her cell and moved towards him, only for movement to attract her attention. With a gasp, she shrank back into the dark, her eyes fixed on the man walking out into the hallway.

Don't see me. Please don't see me.

Bending low, she hugged the shadows of the staircase. Instinct told her to run, but she squeezed her eyes closed and forced that temptation away. Taking a breath, she stayed still where she was. Turning her head, she dared a glance at the man as he walked further into the hallway, his head cocked to one side as if he had heard something. It was the man she had both wanted and dreaded seeing…. Drew Andrews.

It was the proof she needed. Proof that *this* man was the one responsible for what had happened to Chase and for everything that had happened in the house. Now that she'd seen him, they didn't need to stay here any longer. She and Chase could make a run for it – just so long as Drew headed back into the kitchen.

Pressing her lips tight together, Veronica controlled her shaking as best she could. Drew's footsteps were slow, meandering across the hallway as she kept herself back as close as possible to the staircase, grateful for the darkness and gloom that held her. She tried not to breathe, one hand covering her mouth, every muscle burning.

Silence followed. Daring to be bold, she opened her eyes, twisting her head to see where Drew was. He was still standing in the hallway, his arms folded across his chest. He was taller and broader than she'd expected and with enough strength, no doubt, to do whatever he wanted to whomever he wanted.

I can't let him see me.

Her legs were beginning to ache from the fixed position, but she couldn't move away yet. Another flicker caught her attention, and she turned back to see movement near the living room door. It was Chase beckoning to her again. She put a finger to her lips, letting her eyes slide across to where

Drew stood, but she didn't know if Chase could see her in the darkness.

After a second or two, Chase nodded, then pointed toward the front door.

I don't understand.

Her eyes flew wide as Chase disappeared.

What is he doing?

A sudden sound from the living room had Drew spinning around to face the door. He made straight for it without a pause, yanking open the door so hard it cracked back against the wall – and Veronica took her moment to escape. Chase had given her a chance by causing a distraction that would let her run from the house, and despite the fact she was abandoning him in the same room as Drew, she had no other choice.

Go! Go, now!

Her feet propelled her to the front door, sliding through it quickly and pulling her cell phone from her pocket. With shaking hands, she pressed 911 and began the call.

"I need help, please! I'm at the old Draper House. It's an emergency."

The voice at the end of the line asked her what was going on, telling her that someone had been dispatched, and Veronica spoke quickly, sucking in great breaths of cold air, barely aware of just how much she was shaking.

"There are intruders at the old Draper House. The man who owns it – Chase – he's still inside. I don't know where –"

Someone grabbed her shoulder. She spun, her smile spreading, ready to fling herself into Chase's arms in relief... only to realize that it was none other than Drew Andrews.

"Who are you?" His hand reached for her again as she stumbled back. "What are you doing here?"

Veronica shuddered, slipping her cell phone into her pocket as he grabbed her arm. "Get your hands off me."

Drew grinned darkly, his dark eyes flashing with hints of silver as he tilted his head. "Wait, you're the one who sold this place. I recognize you from the brochure."

Waggling one finger, he began to advance as Veronica backed away, not sure where she was going or how she'd escape, but trying to put as much distance between him and her as she could. "You should have sold this house to me. None of this would have happened otherwise." Drew's jaw jutted forward. "You *could* say this is all your fault."

Veronica sucked in air, dizziness threatening as she tried not to let fear grab control of her senses. If she gave in, then she would lose herself altogether. She needed to think, needed to try and find a way to force him to confess what it was he had done...*before* he killed her.

I've got to try to stay alive.

A shaking breath ran out of her lungs. "I don't understand you, Drew." Watching his eyebrows lift in surprise over the fact she knew his name, Veronica forced the words out, ignoring the instinct that told her to run. "Why did you do all of this? What is it about this house – your *uncle's* house – that you want so much?"

His lip curled into a sneer. "Nosy little thing, aren't you?" His eyes narrowed. "What was your name again? Victoria?" Tilting his head, a flash of awareness came into his eyes. "That's it," he snapped, "Veronica. Well, Veronica, I gotta say, you sure know a lot about me."

Trying to put on a show of strength, even though her heart was pounding so loudly she was sure he could hear it, Veronica planted her hands on her hips. "And I know you won't stop until you get what you want, right?" She saw his mouth pull into a hard line. "What is it you've been doing? What is it that you want?"

Drew sneered at her. "And here I thought you'd figured everything out already! What is it that you don't know, Veronica? You've figured out that Mr. Draper was my uncle. You know I want this house, and you know I'll go to any lengths to get it."

"This is Chase's house. He bought it."

Watching her for a second, Drew let out a harsh laugh, and the sound grated across her skin. "Except you should have sold this place to me. Then your precious *Chase* wouldn't have got hurt."

Veronica licked her lips, refusing to be cowed. "And if you had just gotten the paperwork in correctly – and on time – then none of this would have happened."

The man's lips flattened as though she'd deliberately hurt him. "Except I was never going to be able to, was I?" Anger darkened his features, sending shadows across his face, and Veronica's skin crawled. "My uncle made sure of that – and *you* didn't think twice about selling it to someone else." His voice had dropped low as he stepped closer to her again. "And he should have given it to me when I asked for it."

What's happened to Chase? Veronica's eyes darted to the house door as panic began to flutter like a bird in her chest. What if Drew had seen Chase in the living room? What if the worst had happened?

"I'm not going to let anyone get away with what's mine." Drew's voice demanded her attention. "Which means no one gets to step in my way."

Terror gripped her, her whole body tense and primed for flight. Drew's hand went to his waistband, and Veronica's breath left her. She didn't have to try and guess what was in there.

I'm sorry, Chase. Finding the last bit of strength, she lifted her eyes to his again. "So what? You're going to kill me in front of the neighbors?"

He barked laughter. "No one else knows I'm here, so I guess it doesn't matter where it happens."

Shaking violently, Veronica was forced to drop her gaze. "So you'll deal with me the same way you dealt with your uncle." Her voice was trembling, and it was hard to get the words out. She knew she was taking a risk, guessing at the truth, but she had to try.

Drew's shoulders dropped low, his eyes narrowing as he glared at her. Then, both to her horror and relief, he shrugged as if to say that, yes, what she said was true.

"I'm good at getting what I want from people, Veronica. Can't you understand that? My uncle took my money from me – *my* money – and then threatened me. I wanted to go one way with our little business, and he wanted to go the other. *He* wanted to hold onto the power, to tell me where to go and what to do, but I wanted freedom. *I* wanted to call the shots. I'd been listening to him for too long – but oh, no, he didn't like that – and then he was dumb enough to think his threats would work."

Drew's shoulders drew back, his head lifting as if he was proud of what he had done. "I told him I would get back what was mine, that I wouldn't let his threats hang over me – and I was right, wasn't I?" A wry smile pulled across his lips, and Veronica shuddered, hating what he was telling her. She wanted to cover her ears and push away every word, but she *had* to hear this. It was the only way.

"He didn't think I would do it," Drew continued, looking away as if lost in thought for a second. "But I did. I warned him, of course." He looked back at her sharply, and Veronica swallowed hard. "I did give him a chance. I told him he had to tell me where everything was, otherwise, there would be consequences. I told him that, even if he was dead, I'd find a way to get back what was mine – and he didn't believe me. So I did what I had to."

Veronica closed her eyes. "You pushed him down the stairs."

Drew shrugged again as if it was no big deal to have caused the death of his uncle. "Like I said, I had to follow through with my threats. And all the money, all the stuff that belongs to me – it's somewhere in this house. There's no way a man with his past would *ever* trust the bank... or trust the police." A broad grin spread across his face as nausea rolled in Veronica's stomach. "Plus, I've found what I've been looking for. All I need to do now is clean up."

Her hand went to her mouth. *He's not talking about the plaster.*

"A wall will have collapsed onto Chase – an unfortunate accident, of course. That's what happens during renovations." Looking at her, he narrowed his eyes just a little. "But I suppose you're right. You *are* a bit of a problem – what with all these neighbors. I'm afraid you might just have to disappear, Veronica."

Not everything he said made sense to her, but one thing was clear enough. If she didn't do something, if she didn't act, then she was going to die. Drew wasn't going to hesitate, which meant she had only a few seconds to think of something – anything – otherwise, she'd end up just like Mr. Draper – *or Chase*. Closing her eyes for a moment, she drew in strength, finding every last kernel of it she could.

"The police are going to know it's you," she hissed. "They're going to know everything."

Drew only chuckled. "Oh, I'm sure they won't."

Veronica waited, praying for the sirens to come through the air as she squinted in search of the red and blue flashing police lights. But in the moonlight and streetlights, all she saw was the flash of Drew's eyes.

"I've gotten away with plenty of things – theft, assault, murder. Sure, they've convicted me for a few things, but I've grown smarter since then. I know how to escape. I know how to make things look like an accident." With a dark smile, he began to advance, only for Veronica to hold up one hand.

"Except, this time, you've made your confession." Her other hand reached for her pocket, praying what she'd done had made sense, that the operator was still listening, and that the police would have heard everything. "When you were chasing me out of the house, I was calling the police."

The smile faded from his face, a muscle jumping in his cheek as Veronica curled one hand into a fist in an attempt to stop herself from trembling. Any time he wanted, Drew could take out his gun and pull the trigger – even now, even though the cops were coming, in retribution for what she'd done. She had no idea how far his anger would take him.

"I left the line open, and the police have heard everything. The whole conversation." Every word flooded her with a little extra strength. "They heard you admit to killing your uncle, and they've heard you talking about killing me and Chase." Again, her eyes went to the front door of the house, but Chase was nowhere to be seen. "I reckon if you just wait for another few seconds...." Her eyes closed in relief as cop sirens rang through the darkness, winging toward her. "They're coming to arrest you."

All of Drew's bravado was sucked away in the next second. He stared at her, his eyes traveling down to where she held her cell. Veronica glanced at it again, relieved that the call was still going through – that the operator hadn't hung up, and that she hadn't inadvertently pressed the button to end the call when her cell had been in her pocket. Swallowing hard, she forced her gaze back on Drew's face, fixing her eyes on him as hints of triumph filled her, chasing away some of her fear. Sure, he could still pull the trigger. Sure, she might end up lying dead on the street, but at least Drew Andrews would account for his crimes.

"You little –!"

The cars round the corner, screaming towards them as Drew pulled his hand from his pocket. Veronica braced herself, recoiling in fear – just as a huge crash came from the Draper House, and a cloud of dust billowed out the front door.

Chase.

CHAPTER 12

*T*hese guys would never be able to work for me.

Chase pressed his back to the wall beside the door which led to the kitchen. He had no idea where Drew was – or *who* he was, but one glance at the open front door flooded him with relief, knowing that Veronica had escaped and was now calling the police. They'd be here in a couple of minutes, which meant he was going to stand and watch whatever Drew Andrews was up to. The more he could tell the police, the better.

His eyes narrowed.

Except I don't know which one of these guys is Drew.

Chase's stomach knotted. When he'd become aware of someone in the hallway and Veronica hiding in the shadows, the only thing he'd thought to do was to go make a noise in the living room. He'd hidden behind the sofa again – a terrible hiding place but the only one he'd had – and thrown one of his sneakers across the room. It had hit the wall, fallen to the floor, and, much to his relief, had done what he'd intended. The door had opened, and someone – he assumed the man in the hallway – had come in. There had been a few footsteps, and afterward, everything had gone quiet again, but Chase prayed there had been enough time to get Veronica out of the house.

I have to hope she's called the police by now.

"Be careful. We haven't even gotten it all out yet, and I can't risk any of those documents getting damaged."

Documents?

Frowning, Chase rubbed one hand over his jaw. With every movement, his head rang with pain, and he needed to go to the hospital, but right now, watching and listening to as much as he could might be more important than getting himself checked over.

"I think we're going to need the drill. I don't just want to smash blindly into what's left."

Chase winced, edging his gaze into the room again. The half wall, which had been between the kitchen and the dining room, was already partially demolished. Whoever it was hadn't taken the best care. Part of the ceiling was cracking, and a quick glance told Chase that the rest of the wall would collapse soon - and take some of the ceiling with it. It wasn't like he was about to warn these guys about this impending catastrophe, but neither did he want to hang around and witness it.

"We don't need a drill," someone else shouted. "Just give me the sledgehammer."

"We could damage what's left if we –"

"Stop complaining. We don't have long, and Drew's already on our backs." Another voice interrupted the second. "Just give me that sledgehammer and get on with it. We don't have long. Drew said the neighbor is always watching this place. He might end up calling the police."

Chase swallowed hard, sending up a silent prayer that Mr. Jones *had* been watching and had decided to call the police at the same time as Veronica.

I've heard enough.

He'd heard the men talking about Drew concerning money and documents they were trying to get out of the wall. He didn't need to hear more. What he needed to know was how to get out.

Wait.

Before he could move, his breath caught.

Did Mr. Draper put the money and documents into the wall?

It would make sense that he had done it, especially since Drew Andrews had been so determined to buy the house. Groaning quietly, Chase rubbed his eyes as his mind spun. Did it mean Mr. Draper had been killed by his own nephew? Had he refused to tell him where the money was?

Chase scowled. The holes in the wall made sense now. Drew had been looking for wherever his uncle had hidden the money – and now he had found it.

"Stand back!"

The roar from the kitchen had Chase ducking as a small cloud of dust began to billow towards him as the man hit his sledgehammer blow after blow against the wall. Something creaked ominously, and Chase glanced at the ceiling again, then let his gaze swing over to the front door. These guys would knock the whole place down if they weren't careful, and he wasn't planning to stick around while they did it.

Time to go.

With everyone else distracted, Chase made his move. His steps were slow, his head aching with every step he took, but he found his resolve and determination growing through the pain. A little unsteady still, he pushed himself forward in the shadows, one hand leaning on the wall for support. It was only when he reached the door that something erupted behind him. A whirlwind of dust chased after him as creaks and shrieks ran through the house. There were shouts to get out. Staggering forward, Chase made for the door as best he could, forcing one step after the other before a massive cloud of dust propelled him forward.

Something collapsed behind him.

Chase began to cough, gasping for air, and his lungs filled with dust. Somebody was calling his name, and blinded by the plaster dust, Chase stumbled forward in that direction. He couldn't tell whether it was a friend or an enemy, but he had to go somewhere. Dust filled his eyes, his lungs, his nostrils, burning in his throat every time he tried to breathe.

Someone grabbed his hand. "Chase?"

Coughing, his lungs on fire, Chase gripped her hand, knowing at once who it was. He tried to speak Veronica's name, but no sound came out, just another coughing fit.

"Chase, it's okay. Come with me. We have to get you away from here."

"Drew." The word choked from his throat. "Where is Drew?"

She did not answer, instead leading him away, one hand firm on his, the other wrapped around his back.

"Drew?" he said again. *I have to know.* "Is he in the house?"

Veronica glanced up at him as the dust began to settle, the air still appearing a little cloudy, swirling around them. "He's been arrested."

For a second, he sagged against her as relief drowned him. An ambulance came into view, and Chase found himself being led towards it. Soon, strong, capable hands were helping him to sit, putting a foil blanket around his shoulders and someone was checking his airways. Veronica pressed a bottle of water into his hands.

"Drink, Chase." Veronica smiled at him, but even with his blurred vision, he could see how her lips trembled. "I'd better let the paramedics do their job." She stepped back as someone flashed a light into his eyes.

Following their directions, he opened the bottle, exhaustion flooding through him. The cool water touched his lips, and he drank. It tasted better than anything he'd ever had before, and somehow, it seemed to clear his mind a little, giving him back the strength he'd thought he'd lost.

"I'm okay, Veronica," he said.

The paramedic touched the back of his head, looking at the wound, and Chase winced before adding, "They'll get me fixed up, and I'll be as good as new."

"I'm sure you will be." There were tears glistening in the edges of her eyes. "I'm so glad you're safe."

"You're going to need stitches." The paramedic came around to face him, her expression serious. "And I'm pretty sure you have a concussion."

He shrugged. "I figured that would be part of getting hit so hard," he murmured, trying to make Veronica smile, but her expression didn't change. "Are *you* okay, Veronica?"

When she closed her eyes, tears ran down her cheeks. "Drew came out after me." A shuddering breath told him just how frightened she'd been. "He told me everything…. but he told the police as well. I left the 911 call open on my cell and then shoved it into my pocket." Her shoulders dropped. "They've got a recording of it now. Drew admitted to killing his uncle and hurting you. There is nothing he can do now."

"But he could have killed you, too," Chase spoke without thinking what sort of reaction his words would cause. Veronica opened her eyes again and looked straight at him, her face pale in the dim light. "Yes, he had a gun, and for a few moments, I thought he was going to shoot me." She shivered, and immediately, the paramedic came over to her.

"Why don't you come and sit down here?" she said softly, putting one arm around Veronica's shoulders and leading her over to sit beside Chase. "You're in shock. You need to warm up, hydrate, and rest. Don't worry. The team will take good care of you."

"I can't believe he did that." Chase leaned against her as the paramedic settled another foil blanket around Veronica's shoulders. "You have been so brave. I don't think I could have done what you did."

"I'm sure you could have."

"I don't think so." Chase reached out one hand and found hers, feeling just how cold her fingers were. "What you did was incredible, Veronica. To think about doing something like that when you're faced with someone like Drew Andrews? Not many people could have done that."

Her fingers laced through his. "I'm just glad you're okay."

Chase said nothing, looking into her face and finding his heart filling with something new, something unexpected – and despite the circumstances, his face split with a smile. He couldn't talk about it now, of course. It wasn't the time, but there was something about Veronica he didn't think would ever let him go.

And I don't want to let her go either.

"Veronica?"

A woman Chase didn't recognize came over to them. "And you must be Chase. I'm Detective Fields. I've been watching Drew Andrews for some time. I know all about him, and I don't mind telling you we had our suspicions over his uncle's death, although we couldn't prove anything. I can't thank you enough for what you did today. Veronica, your recording and what has happened at this place has made certain Drew Andrews will spend a *long* time in prison." She spread her hands. "But I'm afraid I will need you to come to the station to make a statement. There is a lot we have to unpack here."

"Of course." Veronica's voice was steady and calm, and Chase's admiration for her grew even more. She wasn't buckling, wasn't saying that she needed to rest up, and was begging for the statement to wait for later. She accepted it all, willing to do whatever was required to ensure Drew Andrews was out of their lives for good.

The relief he felt at that was overwhelming, and, with a deep breath, he dropped his head forward for a second, closing his eyes.

"I understand that there was a collapse in the house." Detective Fields indicated the other ambulances which had come up next to their own. "The first responders say three other men are in the house, so far."

Chase nodded. "Drew was out here, but I heard multiple voices in the house. I just can't be sure how many there were."

The detective nodded. "We're going to have to move the rubble to find them, and I'm afraid this house will be classified as dangerous."

Shrugging his shoulders, Chase couldn't find the energy to care. "After all of this, the old Draper house is the last thing on my mind. I'm just glad Veronica is safe, and Drew Andrews won't be able to come back to this place."

"I'm sorry for Mr. Draper." Veronica's voice was soft, her thumb running over the back of his hand. "I'm sorry his life was cut short that way."

"Mr. Draper didn't deserve to die like that." The detective nodded, turning her head away and folding her arms across her chest. "But he had a past – and a criminal record, for that matter."

"What do you mean?" Veronica's eyes widened, her eyebrows lifting. "Are you saying that something was going on between Mr. Draper and his nephew? That they were involved in something nefarious together?"

"That's all I'm saying for the moment. We can talk some more when you come down to the station. We can work through everything then." The detective offered them both a small smile. "Thank you both again for what you did here.

I'm relieved you're both safe, and I hope the hospital can patch you up quickly. Otherwise, I'll see you at the station as soon as you can make it."

"Of course, thank you."

Watching the detective walk away, Chase exchanged a glance with Veronica, then let his gaze drift over to the house. "It seems like the old Draper House held a lot of secrets." He lifted both shoulders. "More than I ever realized."

"Do you regret buying it now?" Veronica leaned towards him, then rested her head down on his shoulder. "It's brought you nothing but trouble, I guess."

"I wouldn't say it's only brought trouble, although it's brought a whole lot of that!" Laughing, he turned his head and pressed a kiss to her forehead, seeing her eyes close. "But it's brought me a lot of good things as well. I'm not going to regret meeting you again, Veronica."

She smiled, sighing. "Does that mean you're going to sell it? Let someone else fix it up?"

"No way." Grinning when her eyes flashed open, a little surprised, he laughed. "When I start a project, I finish it. That's what I intend to do here. This house might have a lot of secrets, but it deserves to be a beautiful, lived-in, happy home. And I'm going to make sure I do it."

Veronica let out a long, contented sigh. "Sounds good to me."

"*A*re you feeling okay?"

Veronica nodded. "I ate at the hospital." She managed a wry smile. "And I fell asleep a couple of times and drank a ton of coffee when I woke up."

The detective grinned. "Understandable." She smiled. "I just talked to Chase, and he seems to be doing okay. If you're up to it, I'd like to hear what you saw. I know you've written a statement, but for clarity's sake, let's go over it again."

"Sure."

"Thank you." Detective Fields took a breath, then shifted a little in her chair. "From what I understand, you were meant to be meeting Chase for a drink at the house."

"Yes, but I was late. I called him a few times, and he didn't pick up, which wasn't like him. Then Bianca – that's my colleague – said something about Drew Andrews, and it was then I found out he was the nephew of Mr. Draper."

Detective Fields nodded. "And you got worried?"

Briefly, Veronica mentioned the previous incidents of finding the holes in the wall and Chase having a near miss. The detective nodded, no flicker of surprise in her expression. She'd read Veronica's statement already and had talked to Chase first, so none of this was new.

"When I came to the house, it was dark, and I was worried about Drew sneaking around. When I crept inside, I heard voices from the back of the house and found Chase in the hallway."

"And you managed to get him into the living room?"

Veronica nodded. "We had to hide in there instead of just heading outside. I thought someone was coming through from the back of the house. We figured we'd call the police from there, but I couldn't find my cell. I'd dropped it when I was trying to get Chase to wake up." The memory seared across her heart, and she snatched a breath, pushing away the menacing tower of emotions that threatened to topple at any time. "Because he was hurt, my first priority was to look after him and get him out of the house – even if he wanted to do the exact same for me. So we figured I'd have to go back into the hall to find my cell."

The detective leaned forward just a little. "And what did you see when you entered the hallway to find your cell?"

Veronica managed a small smile. "Chase was trying to get me back into the living room, but I had to take the chance to see what was happening. I knew that unless one of us *saw* Drew there, the chances of him getting convicted of anything would be slim."

Seeing the detective nod and smile, Veronica ran over everything that had happened. "Drew was going to find me if he came any closer, and that's when Chase made a noise in the living room to distract him. I made a run for the front door and called you."

"It was a good plan."

"And it did work…a little."

The detective's jaw tightened for a second. "Drew Andrews came out after you."

"Yes - and your guys heard every word of our conversation," Veronica finished, feeling a wave of fatigue coming over her. "You heard everything he said to me, how he threatened me, threatened Chase? And how he…" Her eyes closed. "How he killed his uncle?"

"We did." The detective shook her head. "From what we've recovered from the walls, it seems as though Mr. Draper was involved in some of his nephew's more nefarious activities. In fact, it looks like he was more involved than we ever gave him credit for. Even when Drew Andrews was imprisoned, he never said a word about his uncle."

"Family loyalty?"

Detective Fields flashed her a small smile. "Yeah, maybe back then. They must have had some sort of argument more recently because Mr. Draper had money and various documents and photos hidden in the walls of the house – money which Drew Andrews claims is his, but we have no doubt it was stolen."

Veronica nodded slowly, remembering something. "Mr. Jones, the neighbor? He told Chase that Mr. Draper and his nephew used to argue often. Drew told me that Mr. Draper was trying to keep a hold of the power he had, but Drew didn't like that."

The detective nodded. "Drew wanted to take the lead in all of these crimes, but Draper didn't want to let it go, so he threatened him and took away the money Drew would need to try and take charge. We found a significant amount in the wall." Her eyebrows lifted. "A *real* significant amount. Drew would have been crippled." Shrugging, she managed a wry smile. "And it wasn't only money in the walls. There were documents, key evidence that tied Drew to other crimes of which he will now be convicted - some of which go back a decade."

Veronica blinked. "Really?"

"Oh yes." Detective Fields offered her a lop-sided smile. "His uncle knew what he was doing. Upon his death, he detailed that his house went up for sale but with the requirement that the person purchasing the house had to pay in cash. Is that right?"

Realizing what she meant, Veronica caught her breath. "Goodness. So that meant Drew would never have been able to provide me with the missing documents."

"So he could never buy the house," Detective Fields finished for her. "Mr. Draper did everything he could to make certain his nephew didn't get his hands on the money or those documents. Seems to me like he didn't realize how dangerous a man Drew Andrews really is. I don't think he ever expected his nephew would go to such lengths to get what he deemed as his."

Veronica took a long, slow breath, feeling as though every single part of her – both inside and out – was trembling. She and Chase had been so close to something evil and had only just managed to escape.

I don't think I've ever felt so much relief and so much fear before.

Seeing the detective studying her, she managed a small smile. "So what happens now?"

"Well," the detective answered, "we need to process everything at the house. We'll have to go through everything we found and then go over the house again to make sure that we've gathered all the evidence. Some of Drew's men are in the hospital and will be there for a good while, which means we also need to get questions answered and process *them,* but only when they're good and ready. I am sure, however, that Drew Andrews will be easy enough to crack when he realizes he's got nowhere else to go. He's got a lot of bravado but not much courage."

"And what about Chase? When will he get the house back?"

"We'll clear the house as soon as possible," the detective answered. "Whether he's going to want it or not, I'm not sure! The damage to the kitchen, in particular, was extensive. Those guys didn't have a clue what they were doing." She rolled her eyes. "They were just following Drew's orders, I guess."

"And ended up injured because of it."

The detective lifted an eyebrow. "And that's an excellent line for me to use to encourage them to tell me the truth," she mused, a slow smile spreading. "I have to say, I admire how much you've managed to put together. If you hadn't asked Drew those questions and hadn't left the call open, then we might never have been able to catch him with this. You put the pieces together, and because of your bravery, we managed to get the whole conversation." Her eyes glinted. "If you ever want a chance of a career…?"

Veronica managed a dry laugh. "Thanks, but no. Right now, the only thing I want to do is go home and find a way to let myself forget about all of this for a while."

The detective shuffled her papers. "Sounds good. Thank you again for everything. All you have to do now is check and sign your statement, and after that, you'll be free to go."

Veronica let out a long sigh. "Thanks." She picked up the pen, signed her name, and handed the papers to the detective. "Looks like we're done. Guess I won't be seeing you again until before the trial?"

"I'll be in touch about that." The detective stuck out one hand, and Veronica shook it warmly. "Like I said, I think you've got a bit of a knack for this. Just don't let it take you places you don't want to go."

With a smile, Veronica nodded and walked out of the room and out of the station. She had no idea where Chase was, but stepping outside and taking in a huge lungful of the fresh morning air was better than anything.

"There you are."

Chase's warm voice had her turning around, her heart lurching when he smiled at her. The injuries to his head had been stitched, but he'd refused to let them bandage his head. She was just glad to know he was okay.

"Hey." She leaned into him as Chase slipped one arm around her waist, holding her close for a second. "I know it's only been a couple of hours, but it's so good to see you."

Chase's lips brushed her forehead. "I know exactly what you mean."

Sighing quietly, she looked up at him. "You okay?"

"Yeah." His arm slipped back to his side as she stood straight again. "My headache is pretty bad, although part of it is realizing just how much work I've got to do on the Draper house now. It's a much bigger project than I expected." Light danced in his eyes as he grinned. "Although I was planning on demolishing that wall anyway. Maybe Drew did me a favor!"

Veronica laughed, shaking her head. "Very funny." Her shoulders lifted in a half-shrug. "Maybe you'll get some of the money that was hidden in the walls. After all, the property is legally yours. It was sold with all the contents included."

Chase smiled back at her. It was a familiar smile, one that she'd come to know – and love – over the time they'd spent together. "I don't need that money. Even if it does come back to me, I'll donate it."

Her smile fled from her face, her eyes widening. "Are you serious?"

Slinging his hands into his pockets, he kicked at something on the ground, his eyes away from hers. "Like I said, I don't need the money. Plus, if it can be put to good use, then I would prefer that. I don't want any of it for myself."

Taking a deep breath, she looked up at him. *His generosity is overwhelming.* "You know what? I think you're amazing."

Chase turned towards her, his broad smile fading into something more tender. Veronica caught her breath but didn't step back, welcoming whatever was coming her way.

The next second, his arms were around her waist. Her hands slid over his shoulders and around his neck, careful not to touch any part of his head. This felt right. It felt as though they'd been slowly moving toward each other, and now, finally, this was where she was meant to be.

"Right back at you." Chase began to lower his head, and Veronica's heart skipped a beat. "No – much more than that, in fact." One hand lifted from her waist and came to her cheek, his fingers brushing lightly across her skin, sending waves of heat tumbling through her. "I think you are the most incredible, most impressive, most determined woman I've ever met. And the truth is, Veronica, I've never forgotten about our kiss behind the bleachers."

She swallowed hard, barely able to form the words. The intensity of his eyes took all of her strength from her, forcing her to lean into him even more. "I remember it too."

"Then how about we make another memory?"

When his lips met hers, lightning jolted through her. She found her hands tightening about his neck, the soft sweetness of his lips building a fire between them. It wasn't the most romantic of settings – standing outside the police station – but it was everything she'd wanted, all wrapped up in one incredible moment.

"Ouch!"

Chase jerked back, and Veronica dropped her hands, her cheeks burning as she realized she'd run her fingers through his hair. "I'm so sorry, Chase." She reached for him again, only to draw back, mortified. "I forgot about your stitches. I didn't mean to hurt you. I –"

Laughing, Chase winced, then reached out to grab her hand. "It's okay, Veronica. I'm fine." His voice grew a little husky as he pulled her close again. "I'm *more* than okay now that you're here with me like this." Lowering his head, he brushed his lips across her cheek. "We've got plenty of time for all that – perhaps when things are a little more romantic?" Chuckling, he lifted his head to look into her eyes. "I've got another idea for right now."

"Oh?" She couldn't help but smile at how he was grinning at her.

I'd go anywhere with you.

"How about we finally go for that drink? Although, with this concussion, it will have to be non-alcoholic for me."

Her heart exploded as he pulled her tight against him, still grinning as she melted into him, laughing. Her head went to his shoulder, her hand just at his heart. This was the happiest she'd been in a long time, and, at once, all the weariness left her. The mystery of the Draper house was behind them, and the fear and worry swept away.

"That sounds like the perfect end to all of this, Chase." Tilting her head back, she looked up at him, lifting her hand to cup his face, her fingers light against the roughness of his cheek. "There's no one I'd rather spend my time with than you."

"I feel exactly the same way," Chase murmured before dropping his head to kiss her again.

The End

PETALS
OF PERIL

A LAKE MINNETONKA COZY MYSTERY

LYSSA LUND

PROLOGUE

"So, I guess you guys are official now."

Ignoring the small stab of envy that slammed through her heart when Veronica nodded, Sarah tried to smile.

"Yeah, we are." Veronica chuckled, picking up her glass of wine, her cheeks a little pink. "Who'd have guessed I'd have run into Chase so many years later?" She took a sip of her wine. "*And* that he'd still be such a nice guy."

This time, Sarah's sigh caught everyone's attention. Heat built in her face as she waved with one hand. "Don't mind me."

"Oh, but now we're *all* interested." Annie grinned. She tilted her head and swung one leg over the other as she sat back in her chair. "What's got you sighing so heavily?"

"Nothing." Sarah shrugged, but her three friends just looked back at her without saying a word. They'd been friends for a long time, and it didn't look like any of them would believe her. With a groan, she rolled her eyes and set her wine glass on the side table. "I'm happy for you, Veronica. Really, I am. I just wish…" Hesitating, she looked steadily at

Veronica, hoping her friend wouldn't be upset with her for being so honest. "I just wish I had some of your luck."

"I didn't get so lucky the first time," Veronica reminded her with a wry smile. "The divorce was hard."

A stab of guilt pushed its way into Sarah's heart. "Yeah, I remember. I'm sorry."

"Not saying I don't understand." Veronica waved a hand as the other two nodded. "I think we *all* get where you are."

"Except I don't need a man to make me happy," Deborah quipped, making them all laugh.

Sarah grinned. "I get that – and I don't think I need a man to be happy either. I guess I'd just like to meet someone who was actually genuine." Rolling her eyes, she shook her head. "Remember the last guy I dated after I used that dating app? It didn't exactly go well."

"But you shouldn't let that put you off." With a shrug, Annie took a sip of her mocktail. "Plus, that was a long time ago, wasn't it?" Wincing, Sarah let out a laugh. "Don't remind me. It's been *ages.*"

Deborah giggled, and soon, the room filled with laughter. Giving herself a slight shake, Sarah shifted to sit back in her chair a little further. She could always be honest with her friends, and she appreciated that. Deborah was right. She didn't *need* a man to make her happy. She had a lot of happiness in her life already, but seeing Veronica and Chase had made that desire begin to grow again. "I don't know. Maybe I should try dating again."

Her last date had been a complete and utter disaster. Yes, it had been months ago, but still, that memory wouldn't leave her alone.

"Hi!" Her nerves were like butterflies already. So far, Anthony seemed like a great guy, and she had to hope his profile picture was genuine. They'd messaged via the dating app for the last few days before he'd asked her to meet, and ever since she'd said yes, her nerves had been growing. Meeting someone was different from just sending the occasional message.

It's going to be fine, Sarah.

Anthony sounded really good on paper. He'd told her he had a steady job, he lived in the small town next to hers, and that he was looking to start something serious, *if* they hit it off, that was. So she'd agreed to meet him for dinner.

Just gotta pray it goes well.

"Hi there, can I help you?" The girl behind the counter smiled, making Sarah realize she hadn't said anything for a while. "Oh, I'm sorry. Yes, I'm here to meet someone for dinner." Embarrassment caught her throat. *She doesn't need to know it's a blind date.* "Sorry, what I should say is I have a reservation. It's under 'Hayes'."

The girl smiled, nodded, and then looked at her screen for a second. "Oh yes, I see it. Your friend hasn't arrived yet."

"That's okay." Aware she was a few minutes early, Sarah glanced behind her, just in case her date had come in while she was standing at the desk.

No luck.

"Can I order a glass of white wine, please?"

The smile that lifted the girl's mouth made Sarah blush. Okay, she was nervous. *Really* nervous, but maybe she was making that a little too obvious.

"Sure, no problem, I'll have that right over to you straight away. If you would just follow me."

Following the server, Sarah was soon seated at a corner table. The light music quickly eased her nerves, and the wine – which had come immediately definitely helped. The minutes ticked by, and, taking another sip, she took her cell out and set it on the table.

What if he calls to say he can't make it? What if he walks into the restaurant, sees me, and walks right out again?

When ten minutes came and went, Sarah shifted in her seat. She was hot, clammy, and uncomfortable, wondering if everyone in the restaurant was looking at her, wondering why she was sitting by herself. *Maybe I can pretend it's just a modern thing. I'm sure plenty of people come out to eat by themselves.*

Her eyes went to her wine glass.

Except I'm not eating

Swallowing, she licked her lips, thinking perhaps she should just order. He was already almost fifteen minutes late. Maybe he was going to turn out to be a jerk after all.

"Sarah?"

Her mouth was full of wine. She turned, spluttering, then grabbed her napkin to dab at her mouth, her face hot.

"Oh, hi, Anthony." Her eyes slowly took him in. He was tall, with fair hair and a wide smile, wearing jeans and a navy shirt. Her gaze quickly zeroed in on the logo on his shirt. Okay, so he was exactly like he looked in the picture... minus the pizza delivery company logo.

"Nice to meet you." Quickly, Anthony sat down. "I'm so sorry I'm late."

Sarah blinked, slowly withdrawing her hand, which she'd stretched out for him to shake. Something felt...off. "Did you come straight from work?" Silently kicking herself for never asking him what his job was, she forced a smile, stretching it wide.

"Yeah, sort of." Anthony grinned, flashing her a white-toothed smile, his brown eyes warm. His hair was slicked back, but not so much by gel. Sarah wondered if he'd been wearing a baseball cap, which he'd only just remembered to take off. There was a small imprint of a band around his forehead.

I'm not going to judge an appearance.

"I can see you've already started." Lifting one hand, he clicked his fingers in the air, catching the attention of one of the servers. "I'll get a beer, please. Just the one. Thanks." With a grin, he looked at her. "Have you ordered yet?"

"No." Taking a breath, she let her smile fix in place. *At least I'm not being stood up.* "Would you like to order? Here's the menu. I know what I would like."

"I know I would like, too." His smile spread even wider, something flashing in his eyes, but Sarah looked away and didn't return it.

He said he wanted something serious. I'm not here for a one-night stand.

"Pizza?" Before she could stop herself, the suggestion sprang into the air between them, her eyes going to the logo on his shirt again. "Is this what you do for a living?"

"Yeah, I do." His grin turned into laughter as he leaned across the table. "I never get a chance to eat it, though, so maybe that suggestion is a good one!"

Sarah's smile dropped. "Right."

This wasn't what she'd been expecting. Her expectation for the evening hadn't been to sit across from a guy who would drink beer and eat pizza. Grimacing, she looked away from him, only for shame to fall hard on her head. Who was she to judge an appearance? After all, she was the one who had suggested pizza in the first place. They'd hit it off so far over messaging. Perhaps she needed to give it a little more time.

They ordered quickly – he the pizza and she the risotto, and Sarah tried to smile and tried to push away her nagging feelings of doubt.

Anthony took a swig of his beer. "So what do you do?"

"I'm an attorney." Wishing they'd exchanged job details beforehand so she hadn't been so surprised when she'd

111

learned he delivered pizza, Sarah shrugged. "It's a demanding job, but I love it."

"So, what sort of stuff do you do in your attorney job?" His eyes twinkled. "I wonder if you've had to represent any of my friends?"

Her words stuck in her throat, not quite sure if he was joking or not. Thankfully, she didn't have to answer since their food arrived, and all of Anthony's attention went straight to his pizza.

"This looks good, huh?" He picked up a slice without hesitating, only for something to stop him.

His cell phone.

The ringing seemed to echo through the whole restaurant, and Sarah's stomach began to churn. "Sorry. Do you want to get that?" Trying to keep her smile fixed, it waned a little when he shook his head.

"Na, it's okay."

He let it ring, and Sarah cringed at every single chime. She didn't mind if she had his cell phone with him - she had hers too – but surely the least he could do was to silence his notifications for a while. And he definitely didn't need to leave it sitting out on the table like that.

"So, like I was saying –"

For the second time, Anthony picked up a slice of pizza, and again, his cell rang loudly. The jangle clashed with the gentle music around the restaurant, and Sarah winced visibly as a couple nearby turned to stare.

"Sorry." Sighing, he ended the call. "I'm meant to be on my break. I guess they forgot that."

What? Sarah blinked, trying to take in what she'd just heard. "You mean you're working tonight?"

Anthony nodded, biting off a bit of pizza and chewing it furiously. "Yeah, but like I said, I'm on my break." Shrugging, he smiled at her before swallowing the pizza and washing it down with a glug of beer. "That's why I can only have one beer tonight, though. I've only got about an hour."

A slow flush began to climb up her chest, spreading heat up into her neck. "You mean to say you're not planning on spending the evening with me?"

Without even a pause, Anthony shrugged both shoulders. "It's our first date so I didn't think I'd need to."

The heat continued to rise to her face. Was that really how much she meant to him already? The fact that he could only give her an hour of his time — and on an evening when he was working? Hadn't he had any other time free?

"Like I said, it's a steady job." Grinning as if she'd understand, Anthony reached for his beer again. "But from the sounds of it seems like your job is way better than mine. Better paid too, I'd reckon."

"I guess." Talking about her salary wasn't exactly something she had planned to do tonight, but then again, she'd never imagined that a pizza delivery guy would be spending his break with her in a restaurant.

"Maybe you can get the bill tonight, then?" Laughing, Anthony reached across the table and touched his fingers to hers. "Sound good?"

Not for the first time, Sarah was left speechless. Anthony laughed a little more, only to be interrupted by his cell phone ringing again, which was now for the third time.

Exasperated beyond belief, Sarah gestured to it, a tightness about her mouth. "I think you should get that."

Anthony didn't even seem to notice her frustration. Wiping his mouth with the back of his hand, he picked it up and answered the call. "Hello?"

Sarah took another sip of her wine.

"No, I'm on my break, and I'm with someone." He grinned in her direction, but Sarah only took another sip. "What do you mean, overtime?"

Anthony wasn't looking at her anymore. Instead, his eyes were on his pizza, as if wondering whether he could eat as much as he could before his break was up. "But I'm eating right now. And —" His words stopped abruptly. After another few seconds, he sighed, then chuckled. "Okay, okay, you've convinced me. I'll be there in ten."

Surely, he can't be thinking of leaving!

A chill ran through her, embarrassment opening up a gaping hole beneath her, pulling her down towards the floor.

"Looks like we're going to have to reschedule." With no apology in either his voice or in his words, Anthony smiled and then shrugged before looking away. "Let me just...." Snapping his fingers, he caught one of the server's attention as Sarah groaned, closing her eyes tight. "Do you think I can get this to go?"

This would have shocked her if Sarah hadn't been surprised enough already. Instead, she simply turned her head as the server took the pizza away, ready to put it into a box for Anthony.

"I hope you don't mind." Reaching out again, he squeezed her hand, and she tried not to flinch, even though that was her immediate reaction.

"Of course not." *What else was there to say?*

"I'll be in touch. We can do this again sometime. Properly. I mean."

Sarah caught his hand before he pulled away. "No, Anthony." She watched with interest as his eyebrows flew up towards his hairline.

"No?"

"As in, *no*, we won't be doing this again, properly or otherwise." She gave him a small smile. "I don't think we're a good match." Letting go of his hand, she lifted an eyebrow as Anthony scratched his head.

"Oh." Taking a beat, he smiled, shrugged, and then

grabbed the pizza from the server when he brought it over. "Fair enough. I hope you enjoy your risotto. It was nice to meet you."

Sarah held up her empty glass to the server as Anthony walked away. "Would it be possible to get another glass of wine, please?"

The server nodded, smiling back at her. "Sure. And let's put this one on the house, shall we?"

Touched, Sarah managed a nod and a smile before looking back at her risotto. A sense of overwhelming loneliness took hold, and she sucked in air, trying to push it back. Her hopes had been dashed the second Anthony had walked into the restaurant in his work uniform, and he stomped all over her dreams when he'd told her he was on his break. Now, he had decided that overtime was more important than getting to know her.

I sure can pick 'em.

Picking up her fork, she sighed. The very least she could do was salvage her risotto, and she intended to eat it with gusto after all that. Picking up a forkful, a sudden realization hit her, and she froze, her fork halfway to her mouth.

And not only that, he's left me with the bill.

"Sarah, are you okay?"

Pulling herself back into the conversation, Sarah nodded at Veronica. "I'm fine. I was just thinking."

"About?"

With a dry laugh, she rolled her eyes. "About the last person I dated."

"The pizza guy?" Deborah laughed and shook her head. "You gave up dating after that bad date?"

"Something like that." A streak of embarrassment ran through her. "I had one before that, too, remember? The guy just didn't show up. Both of those together really put me off trying the dating scene, especially via any sort of app."

"You just met one – or two bad apples," Veronica said firmly. "If you want to meet someone special, if you really want to make a go of things with someone, then you've got to get back out there. Don't let that bad experience put you off."

Nodding slowly, Sarah picked up her wine again. "I'll think about it."

"Great!" As all three chimed in together, Veronica, Deborah, and Annie shared a look and a smile. Narrowing her eyes, uncertain what they were doing, Sarah looked from one to the other. They were concocting something, she was sure.

"I said I'll *think* about it," she emphasized as all her friends giggled. "That doesn't mean I'm ready to open up that dating app again and start swiping."

Deborah was the one to answer. "What does being ready look like? Either you want to go out on a date, or you don't. From the way you sighed hearing about Veronica and Chase, I'm guessing you're *more* than ready."

A flutter of excitement wriggled in her stomach. "Maybe." Chuckling, she pulled out her cell and waggled it. "I guess that means I'd have to update my profile on that dating app."

"Or we could do it for you."

Before Sarah could say no, Deborah grabbed the cell out of her hand. With a shriek of protest, Sarah got out of her chair to retrieve it, but Veronica and Annie quickly ran over to protect Deborah.

"Come on, at least let us have a look at it for you?" Veronica's eyes were sparkling with laughter. "We know you the best, don't we? We'll be able to get you back on your feet and dating again in no time."

Annie squeezed Sarah's hand. "We promise."

CHAPTER 1

One week later

"What are you guys doing?" Sarah narrowed her eyes as her three friends lifted their heads and stared at her, their faces frozen in innocence as Annie slowly put one hand behind her back. Only a few minutes ago, Sarah had gone to the kitchen to fix a few snacks and had returned to find the three of them clustered together in the living room.

"Nothing."

Sarah waggled a finger in Deborah's direction. "I can tell you're all lying to me, so you don't even *try* to pretend. What are you guys up to?" Tilting her head, she folded her arms across her chest, but her three friends said, "Come on."

It had been a week since her discussion with them about how she'd thought about dating again, and since then, Veronica, Deborah, and Annie hadn't stopped asking her about it. Every time she saw one of them, there had been some mention of it. Deborah had even gone as far as to suggest her cousin as someone Sarah could go out to dinner with, but Sarah had ended that conversation quickly. It was always a bad idea to date a friend's family. There was always the chance things could end badly, with the possibility of losing a friend in the aftermath.

"Well, one of you is going to tell me what you're doing, one way or the other." Hefting her chin, Sarah looked from one friend to the next. "So, come on. Confess!"

All three exchanged a glance, and after another few seconds, Deborah shrugged. "We just thought you might want to try a *new* dating app." Reluctantly, Annie pulled out her hand from behind her back and held out Sarah's cell phone. Stepping closer, Sarah put one hand to her heart, her breath hitching.

"Is that... me?" Aghast, her voice was a thin whisper. "Did you set up a profile for me on this?"

"Yes, we did." Veronica didn't hold back, speaking with as much honesty as usual. "You told us you were thinking about dating again. We just figured you might need a little push in the right direction – and this new app is meant to do great things!"

"This is more than just a little push." Sarah reached for the cell, but Annie withdrew it quickly. "This is a shove!"

"Yes, but look how great a catch you are!" Annie gestured to the screen, still holding it back from her. "*And* we just set you up a few minutes ago, and you've already got a match!"

Indignant flames ignited Sarah's heart, but as Annie grinned at her, they began to flicker and ebb away. "Really?"

Her cell dinged, and Deborah chuckled. "Make that two matches!"

Despite her frustration, Sarah's heart skipped a beat, and, without warning, she took back her cell phone from Annie's hand. "Let me see."

A shiver ran over her skin as she skimmed her profile. She had to admit that her friends had chosen a good photo, but she didn't have time to read everything they'd said about her. Scrolling back to the top, she clicked her 'matches' icon and looked at the first guy and then at the next. "I can't believe I've got two matches already."

"Why? What did you expect?" Deborah smiled and came to stand beside her. "So the first guy is Phillip? He says he's a farmer. And who's the other?"

Sarah clicked on his profile, and Deborah leaned into her, grinning.

"Now, *this* guy is really cute." Her head craned over Sarah's screen. "Look, he works in construction."

"Explains the muscles." Veronica nudged her, laughing as Sarah's face warmed. "What's his name?"

"Steve." Sarah studied the photograph. Steve was square-jawed but with kind blue eyes. He wasn't smiling in his profile picture, but that didn't turn her off. She thought it made him look a little mysterious.

"So what are you going to do." Annie wiggled her eyebrows. "Fancy going on a date with either of them?"

Taking a deep breath, Sarah looked down at the screen again. She ought to be annoyed with her friends for doing this, but the truth was, she was a little glad they'd done it, especially now that she had gotten two matches almost immediately. "I'm not sure."

"What is there to be sure about?" Veronica smiled when Sarah couldn't come up with an answer. "I get that it's scary setting foot back in the dating pool when you haven't done it for a while, but trust me, there's nothing to worry about. All you're doing is going out to dinner or for a drink - and if it doesn't work out with either of them, all you gotta do is go back to the app and look for someone new! You said it yourself, Sarah, you wanted to be with someone. You *want* to find someone special. This is a way of doing that."

Annie smiled quietly as Sarah managed a nod. "I don't think I would ever use a dating app personally, but I think this might work for you." Her head tipped. "What have you got to lose?"

It was a question Sarah couldn't answer. Just looking at Steve, she let her thoughts go back to Anthony, the pizza delivery guy who had ruined her expectations of dating – and to the guy before that who hadn't even shown up.

"Okay."

A smile bloomed on her face, and her three friends cheered and then wrapped their arms around her.

"This is so exciting." Veronica squeezed hard, laughed, and then stepped back. "You *have* to tell us how it goes."

"I will." Already sensing her doubts rising steadily like a floodwater, Sarah turned to Veronica, a sudden hope draining her doubts away. "How would you feel about a double date?"

Veronica's eyebrows shot towards her hairline. "You mean with me and Chase? When you go out with either Steve or Philip?"

She nodded. "Yes, if that would work? I'll definitely feel less nervous that way."

"Then, of course." Veronica smiled warmly. "Try not to worry. I'm sure these two dates are going to go great. Anthony was just a one-time thing."

"I guess." With a smile, she lifted both shoulders. "At least, I have to hope so.

This is bringing me serious déjà vu vibes.

Sarah had no idea why she'd picked the same restaurant as when she'd been out with Anthony, but when Phillip had messaged her, asking her where she wanted to go for their date, she'd panicked and picked the same place as she'd been with Danny. Even the music seemed familiar.

"Hi, I've got a reservation." Her eyes narrowed slightly.

Surely that couldn't be the same girl who had stood behind the counter all those months ago?

"What's the name?"

"Hayes." Sarah lifted her chin, determined not to make any mistakes tonight. She doesn't need anyone here to know she was out on a date... and a *blind* date at that.

"Of course. Right this way."

As they walked, the server looked over her shoulder. "Your friend is here already."

"Great."

Except I don't feel great.

When Phillip had arranged a date for dinner, it was the one night Chase couldn't attend, so she'd had to come alone. Sarah was flooded with nerves, worried Philip would turn out to be someone completely different from what he'd said on his profile. That was the worst thing about dating apps; people could pretend they were someone else.

"And here you are."

The server pulled back the chair for Sarah to sit in, but she didn't move, her feet fastened to the floor. The man who had gotten out of his chair to greet her was definitely *not* the guy she'd expected. This man was about ten years older than her, with thinning grey hair and glasses and without the athletic build he'd posted in his photos.

Oh no.

"Phillip?" Sarah ventured as the server melted away. "You *are* Phillip, right?"

Grinning, he stuck out one hand. "Yes, that's me," he confirmed as Sarah's fears began screaming at her, telling her that her friends had known this would happen.

"You don't look like your profile picture." Not wanting to make a scene by standing in the middle of the restaurant, she placed herself delicately on the edge of her chair.

The man shrugged. "Does it matter?" Still smiling, he sat back down, turning himself to face her. "When I first saw your profile, I *knew* we were going to match. You're perfect for me."

Swallowing, she shook her head. "I don't really like being lied to."

To her frustration, he only laughed. "I didn't lie to you. I just used an old photo, that's all. The only important thing about a person is their character, right?"

Sarah searched his face. Her smile was genuine and she was sure he believed every word – and on the whole, she did too, but then again, she wouldn't have matched with him if she'd known he was so much older than she was. "Do you mind if I ask how old you are?"

Phillip shrugged. "No problem. I'm in my mid-fifties." Chuckling, he leaned across the table towards her, winking broadly. "But I won't be more specific than that."

Surprised, Sarah blinked. She definitely didn't have a problem with someone being a little older, but she wouldn't have matched with someone so much older. After all, she had only just hit forty. The fact he'd lied to her was pushing her away from him. First of all, he'd deliberately used an older photo of himself to appear younger than he actually was. And second, he'd never once warned her about that. It had been a deliberate trick, nothing more.

"Come on." As if he could see her frustration, Phillip reached out one hand, but Sarah didn't offer him hers. "You can't be annoyed with me about that. I'm sure not everything you said in your profile is true."

"Actually, it is." Sarah lifted her chin, glad her friends had decided to be completely honest about everything they'd put in her profile. "I'm exactly who I say I am. My profile picture is from last month."

Phillip's smile faded. "You're not going to hold this against me, are you?" He lifted his shoulders high and held his hands out. "I think you'd be great for me. I'm looking to get together with someone quite quickly, to be honest. A whole lot of work needs to be done at the farm."

The farm?

Blinking, Sarah waved the server away when she came close. There wasn't going to be any need for a drink or even a meal right now. "I'm sorry, Phillip. The farm?"

"Yeah, that's what I said." Phillip grinned at her as if she should already know exactly what he meant. "That part of the profile was true at least."

When he laughed, Sarah didn't join in.

"I mentioned I had a farm, I'm sure," he continued with a smile. "It's a lot of work for one person. My kids all help out, and the oldest one is probably going to take over in the next couple of years, but he'll need all the help he can get. Once he starts running the place, I'll be looking to retire, but I'd want us to stay close to the farm. We could stay here in Excelsior, of course, or think about living somewhere else. If he *does* take over the farm like I hope, then he'd still need us around. An extra pair of hands here and there, you know? And to get plenty of advice from his old man." Chuckling softly, he lifted a shoulder again. "The farm belongs to the family. We'd have to make sure we did all we could to help it thrive for the next generation."

A cold hand gripped Sarah's heart. Somehow, Phillip had gone seamlessly from talking about himself to talking about the two of them together, as if they'd already stepped into a long-term relationship. In his mind, from this moment on, she would be tied to this man and his farm, helping him to settle down into retirement.

Yeah, I don't think so.

"Can I get you anything?"

Phillip looked up quickly. "Oh, I'll have whatever you're having, Sarah."

"I'm not having anything." Sarah managed a brief, apologetic smile. "I'm sorry. Would you mind giving us a few minutes?"

When she looked back at Phillip, his eyebrows had lifted, and his eyes were a little rounded. "What do you mean you're not having anything? My kids won't be here for another ninety minutes."

Sarah dragged in air. "I'm sorry?"

"They won't be here for another ninety minutes," he repeated as if it was perfectly normal for his children to be attending his date. "They really wanted to meet you. I showed them your profile, and after I talked to them about how great it would be for our family, they were all really excited."

This is a disaster.

Struggling to accept all of Phillip's explanations, Sarah took a breath. Why had she ever let her friends talk her into this? "You're going to have to tell them it didn't work out, Philip." Sarah got to her feet, speaking as calmly and as firmly as she could. "I'm sorry."

"You can't leave." In one quick movement, Phillip grabbed her hand, and she hastily turned back to face him, embarrassed to make a scene in front of the other restaurant goers. "We haven't even had anything to eat yet. You don't know anything about me."

Lifting her gaze, Sarah steadily looked back at him, choosing not to say anything, and as the silence grew, Philip seemed to shrink just a little.

He let go of her hand.

She took a breath. "First of all, I know enough to realize that you're not the sort of man I would like to be with. You aren't honest, and I value that trait very highly. You deliberately used an old photo for your profile and pretended to be a whole lot younger than you actually are. Secondly, I have no interest in farming *or* in retiring. And thirdly, I would never expect to meet any of your children until I was in a long-term relationship, and that definitely won't be happening."

Phillip's shoulders dropped as if somehow she had broken his heart by telling him they wouldn't work out. The words, *I'm sorry* came to her lips, but she refused to let them fall. She had nothing to be sorry for.

"I really don't think you're being fair."

"And I really don't care what you think." Aware she was being a little harsh, Sarah grabbed her bag. "Goodnight, Philip. Please don't message me again."

With a toss of her head, she strode to the door, pulled it open, and walked out of the restaurant. Instead of going home, she swung into the nearest bar, her spirits sinking low. Finding a stool, she perched on the edge, pulled out her cell, and waved one hand in the barman's direction.

"Hi."

Sarah looked up at him, a heaviness gripping her as she sank onto her seat. The barman was drying a glass, but one eyebrow was cocked in her direction. He had sharp, angular features with dark eyes that glinted with interest when he smiled at her. "What can I get you?"

With a shrug, she grimaced. "Whatever is going to help me forget about what just happened."

"You sure about that?" The barman grinned, but Sarah struggled to smile back. "You might pay the price for that tomorrow."

"At this point, I don't care."

"I see." His smile was a little softer than she'd anticipated, and she was sure there was a glint of sympathy in his eyes. "That bad, huh?"

"The worst." Cocking her eyebrow, she tried to smile, but it broke into pieces. "So what should I have?"

"Well, what's your usual?"

Tilting her head, she thought for a moment. "I'm usually a white wine or a rosé."

"I've got that here." Gesturing behind the bar, he grinned back at her. "So how about a couple of shots to take the edge off, and then you go for your usual? That way, you won't regret it in the morning."

Sarah smiled at him, the sharp pain of meeting Phillip finally fading. "I thought you guys were meant to try to get as much liquor down your customers as possible."

Laughing, he pulled out a shot glass and sat it in front of her. "I'm not most guys."

"I can see that." Picking up the shot, she slugged it back, then set it down again, fighting to catch her breath as heat enveloped her chest. "Another." The word shot out in a half-gasp, half-shout and the barman grinned but obliged.

"I'll go get you that wine." While his back was turned, she picked up the second shot and threw it back, feeling the tension began to ebb. Her shoulders dropped and she wiggled them lightly, smiling appreciatively when he set down a rather large glass of rosé in front of her.

"It's pretty quiet in here tonight." The barman gestured to the half-empty bar. "You've got my full attention if you want to tell me what's going on."

Sarah's tongue ran lightly over her lips. Was he just being friendly, or was it something more? "Are you sure you want to hear about the worst date ever?" She held up one hand, silencing him before he could say anything. "Do you want to hear about the worst *two* dates of my life? In all honesty, it's quite a sad story."

To her surprise, he put out the hand over hers for just a second. "I'm good with sad stories." A wry smile lifted his mouth. "I've had a fair share of them myself."

"If you're sure." When he lifted his hands, heat ran

through her as if he'd left something hot behind. A smidge of interest had her curling her toes, and when he dropped his tip at the counter, his dark eyes fixed solely on her, electricity pushed itself through her veins as she smiled back at him.

Perhaps this evening was going to turn out better than she'd expected after all.

Ready to find out what happens next?

Continue reading Petals Of Peril here.

AFTERWORD

Thank you for reading my books! I know you have so many choices and I am honored you have chosen to read mine.

As an independent author I really depend on your reviews to help new readers take a chance on my work. If you enjoy Petals Of Peril it will help so much if you can take a few minutes to leave a review.

Amazon is preferred if it is possible for you to do so. Goodreads and Bookbub are helpful too.

Happy reading!

xoxo, Lyssa

ALSO BY LYSSA LUND

Shadows Of Dark And Light

A Touch Of Prophesy

The Dark King's Heart

The Sylvan Wilds

The Borderland Guardians

The Blizzard Crossing

Beyond Aorel

Realms Of Destiny Series

The Lost Heir Of Isla

Kingpin Of Topree

Maya Rodgers Mysteries

Deadly Dynasty

Ink and Blood

Brushed By Danger

Lake Minnetonka Cozy Mysteries

Secrets Buried

Petals Of Peril

ABOUT THE AUTHOR

About Lyssa Lund

Lyssa Lund discovered her love of reading in first grade when she discovered Hans Christian Anderson and The Brothers Grimm fairy tales.

Lyssa is an avid reader and writer who understands wanting to escape and be carried away by the story. While keeping it clean, Lyssa aims for the best in strong female characters, heart-of-gold alpha heroes, mystery, suspense, and heartwarming romance.

Lyssa lives in the upper midwest, where the winters are long and cold and perfect for reading and writing by the fire. She shares a home with her wonderful husband and two Borzoi hounds.

She adores reader feedback at hello@lyssaLund.com.

Find out more about Lyssa at lyssalund.com